Muscle Cars

STEPHEN G. EOANNOU

www.sfwp.com

Library of Congress Cataloging-in-Publication Data

Eoannou, Stephen G.
  [Short stories. Selections]
  Muscle cars / Stephen G. Eoannou.
    pages cm
    ISBN 978-1-939650-22-1 (trade paper : alk. paper)
  I. Title.
  PS3605.O16A6 2015
  813'.6—dc23
                                      2014025044

Published by SFWP
369 Montezuma Ave. #350
Santa Fe, NM 87501
(505) 428-9045
www.sfwp.com

Cover photo: Jody Potter

Find the author at www.sgeoannou.com

Contents

For my father, who always loved a good story.

From passing cars, voices sing out

None But The Brave
Bruce Springsteen

Muscle Cars

Originally published in *The Barely South Review*

I have trouble sleeping.

The headlines keep me awake: another bombing in Iraq, the Taliban resurging in Kandahar, more attacks in Fallujah.

My wife can't sleep, either.

"He's at it again," Maureen says, lying next to me.

"Bin Laden?" I ask, squeezing my quadriceps together, forcing blood into the muscles. "We got him."

She props herself on an elbow. "Scotty," she says. "From next door."

I cock my ear toward the window and hear the cars rumbling in front of the house; they're the same ones that show up every night loaded with kids: a Cutlass with a prom garter hanging from the rearview mirror; a blue Chevelle with growling cherry pipes; and a beat up Camaro, its quarter panels primed black.

They're muscle cars, the type of car my brother Gregg and I have always loved.

"Every night, the same thing," Maureen says.

Scotty and his friends race their engines before shutting them off, filling the night with exhaust that drifts through our bedroom window. Then I hear car doors banging and laughter. Scotty's screen door slams and slams and slams until they're all in the house, and then the music starts, the volume not quite loud enough to make out a specific song but turned up just enough so we can hear the thumping bass.

"This is ridiculous," she says.

Maureen kicks off the sheet, rolls out of bed, and shuts the window. I've asked her countless times to lift weights with me in the garage, but she always shakes her head and looks at me strangely. She thinks I'm crazy because I spend all my free time amongst the old tires, lawn mower, and gardening tools, pushing more weight than I should without a spotter.

The hard work is paying off. I'm in the best shape of my life, ready for whatever's thrown at us.

"I'm sick of it," she says, climbing back into bed. "The cars, the music, the yelling when they finally leave. And I know someone's been peeing on the flowers. The roses reek of urine."

"Come on, Mo. We used to party when we were kids."

"Not every night. Enough is enough, Tom." She pauses for a moment, and I imagine the gears grinding in her head. "Tomorrow I want you to talk to him."

I lie very quietly, flexing my quads, trying to make out the music coming from Scotty's house.

"Did you hear me, Tom? You need to talk to him."

"Okay."

"I mean, this is crazy. I'm not getting any sleep, are you?"

"No," I say, and think of insurgents, car bombs, and IEDs. "They're just kids, Mo. Let them be kids as long as they can."

"Explain things to him, Tom. You're good at that," she says, and I wish that were true.

She rolls away from me.

I hadn't said more than hello to Scotty since he moved back into the house. Last summer, a drunk driver killed his mother. She died instantly; there was a newspaper article about it. Scotty went and lived with his father somewhere in the suburbs, but his dad had a new wife, a new life, and twin girls.

It was about this time that I built the gym in the garage. I made my own squat rack and preacher curl bench and bought an Olympic weight set off a kid heading to Parris Island. I bolted a chin-up bar to the wall and began reading muscle magazines filled with bodybuilders so knotted with muscle they looked cartoonish. At least once a week I measured various parts of my body, and Maureen began whispering on the phone with her mother.

Scotty's house remained empty next to ours. The driveway and sidewalk went unshoveled and drifted over in the winter, and last spring the melted snow revealed all the unraked leaves from the previous fall. The grass grew ankle-high before Scotty showed up to mow it. Last week he turned eighteen and moved back in the house.

The parties started soon after.

By this time I had transformed.

My body is hard and muscled, tapering to a 'V' at my waist. I cut my hair shorter so my face looks wider and my neck thicker. The veins in my arms and across my chest stand out like fire hoses. Sometimes I feel like I can lift the whole house, Maureen and all, right off the damn foundation.

The next morning, I lie in bed, flexing various muscle groups, gauging my soreness from the previous day's workout. I hear Maureen moving around in the bathroom, humming to herself. Then it becomes very quiet and a moment later the bathroom door slowly opens.

"Is this yours?" she asks, standing in the doorway.

I nod, recognizing the plastic bag immediately.

"What is all this stuff?" she asks, walking toward me and dumping the contents on the bed. "Anti-bacterial soap? A home waxing kit? Razors? You don't plan on…are you going to shave your *legs*?"

"And my chest and arms," I answer. "I don't think I have any on my back, do I?" I roll on my stomach.

"Why? Why would you do that, Tom?"

"All the bodybuilders shave," I say, turning back to face her. "I don't want hair covering all the muscles and veins. I want them to see what they're messing with."

I get out of bed and start putting everything back in the bag.

"Who, Tom? Who's *them*?"

"Don't worry about them. I'll take care of you." I kiss her cheek as I walk past her to the bathroom.

As I shut the door, I hear her dialing.

I arrange all the items from the bag on the sink. Using a razor seems simpler than waxing, so I start with my arms, only nicking myself once near the elbow. When I finish, the skin feels smooth and the arms look thicker, meatier, more intimidating. I had stopped at the wrist, but the contrast between the smooth arms and the hairy knuckles looks odd, so I shave the backs of my hands and fingers before starting on my thighs.

Maureen knocks on the bathroom door. "Tom? Are you all right?"

I look down at my legs. They're pink and irritated; blood trickles from my left ankle to my heel.

"I'm fine, hon," I say, lathering my chest.

"I'm going grocery shopping, okay?"

"Okay."

"Don't forget to talk to Scotty, all right?"

"I'll take care of it." I remove a patch of chest hair with a single, clean stroke. "You can count on me."

The Camaro is parked in the driveway, still pinging hot when I cut across my lawn towards Scotty's house. The Chevy's tires are worn smooth, and a crack webs across the windshield. Jumper cables lay tangled on the backseat. I walk to the back of the house and peer through the screen door. Beer cases are stacked by the refrigerator, an open pizza box sits on the counter, and plastic garbage bags stuffed to bursting stand near the basement steps, waiting for someone to carry them out. From deep in the house I hear *The Doors*.

I knock, but no one answers, so I knock harder. The music stops, and footsteps pad up the basement stairs. Scotty's friend, the owner of the Camaro, appears at the door. I've seen him around before. He wears a black leather vest over a black T-shirt with Megadeath written in dripping red letters. His hair hangs long and straight to his shoulders.

His eyes widen when he sees me. "Hey."

"Hey," I reply. "Is Scotty around?"

"Let me check," he says, and heads down the basement. "It's the weird guy from next door," I hear him say.

They murmur together before the kid comes back. "Scotty says you can come down."

He unhooks the latch and leans away from me as I squeeze past. The smell of spilled beer and marijuana grows stronger as I head down the stairs; potato chips crunch under my feet. Posters—Janis, Jimi, Jim Morrison—hang on the basement walls. Empty beer bottles and cans are scattered on the floor. Scotty sits shirtless in the middle of a sagging leather couch, his soft belly hanging over his Hawaiian shorts. The florescent ceiling lights reflect off his round John Lennon glasses.

"Mr. Mastoris," he mumbles, then tilts his head towards a beanbag chair in the corner. "Have a seat. That's CJ over there."

I nod to the kid in the black vest, who sits on the bottom step. I sink in the beanbag, my knees to my chin.

"Can I get you something?" Scotty asks, and then looks at CJ. They start laughing, both stoned already. Wake and bake.

I smile, shake my head, and point to the posters. "You need some pictures of survivors. Those guys didn't make it."

"Break on through, man," CJ says. "One of these days me and Scotty are going to Paris and visit Morrison's grave. You ever been there?"

I shake my head. "I've never been to France."

"Where you been, besides Iraq?"

"CJ," Scotty says, admonishing him.

"What? What'd I say?"

"I was never in Iraq, either. I was never in the army."

CJ glares at Scotty. "You said, man. You said he was."

Scotty shrugs, his pupils like saucers behind his Lennon glasses.

"What made you think I was in Iraq?" I ask.

Scotty shifts on the couch, the leather squeaking under him. "I don't know."

"You can tell me. I won't get mad."

He laughs, shakes his head, and turns to his buddy for help.

"Well, you know," CJ starts. "You got them war bumper stickers all over your car, and, you know, you kinda act weird."

"Oh, man," Scotty says. "Jeez."

"He asked, didn't he?" CJ turns to me. "Didn't you ask?"

I look down at my legs, razor burned and scabbed where I'd cut myself. "What do I do that's weird?"

Scotty starts rocking back and forth.

"I don't know," CJ says, and then pauses a beat. "You talk to the newspaper."

Scotty laughs as he rocks.

I smile. "I what?"

"You talk to the paper. Every night we see you. The paperboy throws it on your porch, you come out, sit on the front steps, and start reading. Then your hands shake, and we hear you talking to it. Sometimes you throw the pages down and walk around the yard, kicking at the grass. But you always go back and pick it up and do the same thing over and over again until you read the whole thing. Then you go into the garage and start lifting weights and groaning and tossing dumbbells around. It's funny."

"Yeah, it's funny, Mr. M," Scotty says. "No offense, but it's real funny."

They laugh together.

"That must look pretty weird," I say, deciding I could press both of them over my head if I had to.

"So, you really weren't in Iraq?" Scotty asks. "All the guys think you have a drawer full of medals and guns and stuff. They're all afraid of you."

Not afraid enough to stop peeing on Maureen's roses, I think.

"No," I say, instead. "I wasn't there. My kid brother Gregg went. He wasn't much older than you when he enlisted. I tried talking him out of it, but he had his mind made up. " I turn to CJ. "He'd drool if he saw your Camaro."

"Yeah?"

"He started working on cars when he was a kid. Yours would be a challenge to him. He'd want to fix it up, maybe put some big mag wheels on the back or a spoiler. You should see the before and after pictures of the GTO he restored."

"Convertible or hard top?" CJ asks, leaning forward on that bottom step.

"Two-door hard top. Cardinal red."

"Sweet." CJ grins at me.

I nod. "He got lousy grades and was always in and out of trouble, but he was good with tools. That old Pontiac didn't even turn over when he bought it. I told him he was throwing his money away, but Gregg never listened to me. He kept working on it and working on it. He even did the bodywork himself. She runs a little rough, but she's a beauty now."

"You think he'd look at the Camaro for me? You know, give me some ideas?"

"No."

"Can't you just ask him? He might say yes."

I shake my head.

"I'm a quick learner, dude. I just need someone to show me."

"Gregg's dead."

Scotty rocks faster.

"He was killed by a roadside bomb outside of Basra. One of the guys in his unit, a kid named Tyler from Wyoming, survived the blast and wrote me. He said one minute they were riding, laughing about something, and then he heard a pop, then darkness. There was scream-ing, but he doesn't think it was Gregg. Tyler was covered in blood and engine oil. Isn't that weird? Engine oil? I never imagined that would happen, but I guess it makes sense. Gregg didn't have any oil on him, which is ironic since he always seemed covered in grease when he was home and working on his cars. He was thrown six feet from the vehicle and their five-hundred-pound gun turret landed on him. Tyler thinks he died right away, probably didn't even know what hit him. But who knows about a thing like that?"

I hear Scotty breathing hard, his nose whistling when he exhales.

"When?" he asks.

"About a year ago."

"That's when my mom died."

"It happened right after."

Scotty sags into the couch like he's deflating. Maybe he pictures himself and CJ riding in an armored vehicle or on foot patrol in an Iraqi market. Then a pop, or possibly a louder explosion, the kind that can level vendor stalls and adjacent homes.

Maybe he imagines CJ blown in half or crushed by a fucking gun turret, and realizes that if this happened they'd never again pass beer or joints to each other while their muscle car roars. Or maybe he's just thinking about his mother and how he can fill her house with people and music every night, but the place still feels empty.

One thing is certain as I sit in that beanbag chair. I had told a real story, one they might read in the newspaper, and the rawness scares them. Both boys shift around, their eyes looking everywhere but at each other. I can tell they don't like the helpless feeling that grips them. Like me, they want something solid to hang onto, something to make them feel safe and in control.

CJ and Scotty aren't bad kids.

They're just lost.

They need someone who's been around and knows the score, someone to spend time with them and help them find their way. Who is more qualified than I am to save these kids? This time, I'd think of all the right arguments. I'd drive home that one convincing point that would keep them riding on the right road.

This time, I'd get it right.

"Mr. Mastoris," Scotty asks, as he reaches over and flips on the stereo. "Why did you come over today?"

As the music pushes me deeper and deeper into that beanbag chair, I flex my muscles, think of Maureen and these kids, but can't, for the life of me, remember.

.

Mementos

Originally published in *The MacGuffin*

've been in the funeral home, an old Victorian with a domed turret on High Street, exactly three times: once when my grandfather died, then again when my mother passed away, and now I had come back from my home in Albany to bury my father.

I'd made most of the funeral arrangements over the phone before I drove back, deciding that it made sense to have my father laid out in the former parlor, the smallest of the reposing rooms; my father had out-lived most of his family and friends. My mother, aunts, uncles, and all the old Greeks who had sat around the counter at my father's restaurant had passed on before him. I wasn't sure if anyone other than my Uncle George and a stray cousin or two would even show for the wake.

When my Uncle George arrived, an aide from the home wheeled him to the coffin. He had lost weight since the last time I visited. His clothes and sallow skin hung off him in folds. We were not blood related; my father had always called him his 'Left Tit Cousin'. Both men were born in a small village on the Greek island of Evia. For whatever reason, George's mother was unable to breastfeed her baby, so my grandmother nursed both boys.

"Uncle George," I said, and bent down to hug the old man in his chair. He patted my back as if the bones in his hands were fragile and would shatter into brittle pieces.

"Christos," the old man rasped, his voice damaged from cigars and surgeries. "Your father always was ahead of me."

"What are you talking about?" I asked, pulling a chair next to him. "You look like you'll outlive us all."

Uncle George shrugged, then glanced around the empty room, taking in the unoccupied chairs lined in rows before the casket. "You're alone."

"It's early. Some people may still show."

Uncle George looked at me with filmy eyes. "No, I meant where's your wife? Where's Jenny?"

"She has a trial. She couldn't get away."

Uncle George shook his head, his white hair so thin and wispy I could see his spotted scalp. "Not even for this?"

"It's an important case. She's on the news almost every night," I said.

Another elderly man approached the casket to pay his respects, leaning heavily on his cane as he limped toward the bier. He saved me from fumbling through another explanation of why I'd made another trip home without my wife. Jenny was a top defense attorney, and her career had always come first. I told people I was proud of her.

The man finished praying in front of the coffin, made the sign of the cross Orthodox fashion, right to left, and then turned to us. He smiled, showing us missing teeth.

I extended my hand when he got close. "I'm Chris, Gus's son."

The old man introduced himself as Tony but said Dad had always called him 'Shoes' because of the stolen bowling shoes he wore during the Depression. He studied my face. "You look like him. Just like him."

It's true. I'm a younger version of my father, having inherited the same heavy-lidded eyes that give me a melancholy appearance even when I laugh, the same olive complexion, the same dark curly hair that started streaking silver when I was in my twenties.

"Your father was a good man," Shoes said. "I still tell stories about the restaurant and the people there—Lefty the Gambler, Jimmy the Popcorn Man, and all those damn Irish cops wanting to eat for free."

"Don't forget Happy Harry. What a miserable man. Never had a kind word to say about anybody," George added, staring across the empty funeral parlor as if they were all standing there, waiting their turn to say goodbye to my father or, perhaps, to welcome him.

I don't tell stories about Lefty or the rest of them. I remembered them differently, as loiterers wreathed in hazy cigarette smoke, drinking endless cups of free coffee and putting very little into the cash register.

"And Laura," Shoes said, turning to me. "My God, how your father loved her."

"My mother's name was Helen."

Shoes shook his head. "It was always Laura."

Uncle George looked away.

A cold rain fell the day of the funeral, and the weather kept the older people home. We were short two pallbearers, so the owner of the funeral parlor and his son, James and James Junior, had to fill in. It was a small group graveside as the priest hurried through the final prayers. We all carried umbrellas except James Junior. With the spring shower soaking him, he stared across the cemetery as if thousands of miles away, visualizing an entirely different scene. He'd been wounded and discharged from the Marines a year ago, but he still kept his hair high and tight.

After the priest gave the final blessing, everyone scattered as fast as they could, and I was left alone by the open grave, the rain beading the top of Dad's coffin like a freshly waxed car. My father was buried next to my mother in the Hellenic Gardens, the portion of Elmlawn Cemetery the church had bought decades ago for all the Greeks to lie in rest together.

I wandered the cemetery, reading the headstones in the rain. I recognized the names—Triantafilou, Pappas, Alefantis—and sometimes was able to conjure faces to go with them. At some point, I found myself searching for a marker with the name Laura cut into it, but this was not a place where Lauras slept. The women buried here were named Despina, Chrisoula, Helen.

~

After the funeral, I went by the nursing home to sign the final papers and collect my father's belongings. My wet shoes squeaked down the antiseptic halls as I carried the boxes to my car. There wasn't much to sort through when I got back to my hotel on High Street, just blocks from the funeral parlor. There were a few books, some framed pictures of my parents, a picture of me and Dad from last Christmas, and a faded Polaroid of my grandfather, my father, and me at maybe five years old, standing in front of the cash register—three generations of restaurant men. As I grew up, I realized I wanted no part of the restaurant, of the endless hours behind the grill, of trying to make ends meet, of being married to the damn place. I'd moved to the other end of the state to make sure I wouldn't be pulled into that life out of guilt, or family obligation, or lack of options.

His clothes would all be donated to AMVETS, so I sorted through those quickly, setting aside his worn Greek fisherman's cap and favorite wool sweater for myself. At the bottom of the clothes I found a humidor, one I didn't remember seeing at the house growing up or at the nursing home when I had visited him. It was old, made of red mahogany with brass corners, the patina rich and warm. The box was locked. I searched through my father's possessions for the key, finally finding it on his old brass ring that still held his army dog tags and the keys to our house and restaurant, both buildings long sold.

The humidor opened easily, as if the lock had been used on a regular basis. Setting on top of some black and white photographs was a gold, square-faced Bulova with Roman numerals at the quarter hour. The watch was heavy, substantial. I had never seen it before. I turned it over and read the engraving on the back:

Welcome Home
Xmas 1945
L

I wound the stem and it began ticking; I set the time and slipped it around my wrist. The photos in the box were of my father and a woman I didn't recognize: the two at the beach, smiling behind sunglasses; her on a stool at the restaurant, her legs crossed and her skirt pulled above the knee; another of my father, impossibly young in his army uniform with his arm around her waist, pulling her close as they posed in front of a fountain. There was nothing written on the backs of the pictures—no dates, no places, no names—but I assumed the woman was Laura.

There were a few other items in the humidor: a matchbook from the Calumet Club and another from the *Chez Ami*, "Home of the Revolving Bar"; ticket stubs from the Allendale and Granada theaters, both razed when I was a kid; a circus handbill from July 25, 1942 when Barnum and Bailey had come to town.

And an engagement ring.

The ring was made of platinum, or perhaps white gold, and made to fit a slender finger. The large diamond in the middle reflected the hotel room's lights and was offset by smaller, single-cut diamonds on either side. I held the ring between my forefinger and thumb appraising it, trying to calculate the implications and the heartbreak that it held. I thought I knew everything about my father. I'd heard his stories about the Depression and the war and the restaurant so many times, I sometimes felt as if they had become my own. As I closed my fingers around the ring and pressed it into my palm, I wondered about the stories he hadn't told and what other mementos he had kept locked away.

The photo of Laura on the restaurant stool was the clearest shot of her. Her hair was curled, and a section near the crown on each side was pinned off her face. I have some pictures of my mother with a similar hairstyle. She had called the curls "Victory Rolls". Laura's hair was a lighter shade than my mother's. Her skin seemed fair, her eyebrows perfect arches. She was laughing at the camera, her slender fingers curled around the hem she had pulled higher.

I studied the photographs, memorizing one before placing it down and picking up another. I slowly became aware of an unwinding motorcycle engine tearing down High Street, the rider running hard through the gears, and I moved to the window. The rain had stopped and sunlight now reflected off standing water, casting a spectrum of color across the road's oily puddles. A big bike roared past my hotel, the headers wide open, the noise vibrating the windowpanes, its angry Harley sound distinct. At the end of the street, the biker turned around and raced back the other way, this time moving faster, louder. The rider didn't wear a helmet, and I recognized his military haircut as he blurred by.

I stood in the window and watched James Junior rocket up and down High Street, his engine growing louder, more dangerous sounding, each time he shot past. I leaned my forehead against the cold glass, watching him drive back and forth for twenty minutes, and I wondered about Laura and the secrets buried with my father.

The Bulova kept perfect time.

The next day I visited my Uncle George. He was lying in bed, propped by two pillows, his head back, his mouth open, snoring like he was partially submerged. At times, his snoring would halt, and he seemed to struggle for air. When his breathing resumed, there was a rattle in his chest, like something had broken free. Then he awoke with a gasp, startling me, his eyes fluttering open and then darting around the room as if he didn't know where he was or maybe just surprised to still be here. He gasped a second time when he saw me in the chair.

"Gus."

"It's me, Uncle George. Chris."

He fell back into the pillows, exhaling loudly, even his sighs sounding rough. I moved my chair closer to the bed.

George noticed the humidor on my lap. "You brought me hand-rolled Cubans?"

"You smoked White Owls with plastic tips from McClusky's drug store."

"I can't go out in style? Hand me my water."

I held the cup with the matching lid as my uncle leaned forward and took the straw between his papery lips. He leaned back when he was done. "So if they're not cigars, what'd you bring me?"

I handed him the photographs.

Uncle George made a leaking sound then, as if air were seeping from his cancerous lungs and damaged esophagus. He lingered on each picture before flipping to the next, his eyes brimming.

"Is that Laura?" I asked.

The old man nodded, unable or unwilling to speak.

"I found them in Dad's things."

He nodded again, not surprised at all.

"Who was she, Uncle George?"

He closed his eyes, still holding on to the photographs, his bottom lip trembling. "We don't speak of her."

"Did Mom know about Dad and her?"

"Everyone knew Laura," he said, his voice like grit.

"I never heard of her before yesterday."

"We don't speak of her."

"Dad's gone. You can tell me now. What happened to them?"

Uncle George placed the photographs next to him on the mattress and waited a minute, his breathing painful to hear. "She left him," he finally said. "Moved to Saratoga Springs."

"Why?"

"How would I know? It was a long time ago. Leave it alone."

I gathered the photographs and slipped them back in the humidor. "What was Laura's last name?"

"Go home, Christos. Go back to Albany. Go back to your life."

"Just tell me her name, Uncle George. Can't you do that?"

I listened to him wheeze, watching his sunken chest move in and out with each strangled breath. He whispered that she'd married a man named Sheridan.

My wife thought it was silly that I wanted to find out about Laura.

"So your father had a girlfriend before your mother. What's the big deal?" Jenny said, her voice breaking up slightly on my cell phone as I drove east on the thruway.

I gripped the steering wheel tighter. "Because he kept it a secret. Because there was a ring."

"Is she even still alive?"

"I don't know, but I want to find out. I drive right by the Saratoga exit. It won't take me long."

"Okay," she said, and then began talking about her trial. As Jenny spoke, I pressed harder on the accelerator, rushing faster towards Saratoga Springs, not listening to a word she said.

There were three Sheridans—Andrew, David, and Joyce Sheridan-Sinclair—listed in the Saratoga Springs phonebook, but no one named Laura. I left a message on Andrew's answering machine; David had never heard of a Laura Sheridan; Joyce Sheridan-Sinclair was Laura's married daughter.

"You're whose son?"

"Gus Spanos, from Buffalo. Our parents were friends back in the forties," I said, lying on my hotel bed, the phonebook open next to me. Framed pictures of thoroughbreds lined the walls, some in full gallop, others standing looking majestic, their heads raised, their shoulders well-sloped, their hindquarters muscular.

"I don't remember Mother ever mentioning a Gus Spanos from Buffalo. She often speaks of growing up there, especially lately, but she's never spoken of anyone by that name."

I sat up. "She's still alive?"

"Why, yes. I just assumed that you knew that. She lives with me now. And your father?"

"He passed away recently and I found some pictures that I thought your mother would like to have."

Joyce was silent, and I thought the call had been dropped. Then, "I'll ask if she'll see you. She hasn't been doing well the last few days, I'm afraid. Maybe memories from the past will cheer her."

I gave her my cell number and the number at the hotel, and she promised to call me after she spoke with Laura. Lying back in bed, I reached for the photographs on the night stand and stared at the one with Laura's hair pinned up in Victory Rolls, wondering what I'd say to her, how I would form the questions, certain she'd tell me that my father chose my mother over her.

Union Avenue was a broad, tree-lined street with many of the Victorian houses set back from the road. A street of funeral parlors, I thought, as I drove past all the Queen Anne's with their towers and turrets casting long shadows across manicured lawns.

A covered porch ran the front of Joyce's house and wrapped around the side. Just to the left of the carved screen door, two rocking chairs angled toward each other. An old woman sat in one, staring hard at me as I parked in the driveway and made my way to the front steps with the humidor under my arm.

"You look like him," she said, her voice a thin blade.

"I get that a lot," I replied, smiling as I climbed the steps.

She didn't smile back. "But you're not like him at all, are you?"

I sat in the other rocking chair and didn't know how to answer. "I'm Chris," I said.

"I know who you are," she said, and repositioned the blanket that covered her legs, although the temperature had to be seventy degrees.

I didn't expect the girl from the black-and-white photographs to be waiting for me on the porch, but it was hard to find even a trace of that girl in the old woman slowly rocking in the chair next to me. Her yellow-white hair was pulled back in a severe bun, and her skin, so fair and smooth looking in the photos, was now creased and wrinkled like parchment. Her hands, folded on the blanket, were mottled. Only her eyebrows, still perfectly arched, had remained the same.

"My father passed away this week," I said.

She nodded. "George told me."

I sat back in the chair.

"You look surprised."

"George made it sound like he hadn't talked to you in years."

"George has always kept in touch."

"Did my father keep in touch, too?"

Her eyes, gray with flecks of yellow, narrowed. "How much do you know about me and your father?"

"I know you were friends."

She snorted.

I opened the humidor and handed her the photographs. From under the blanket, she produced a pair of glasses and slid them on. For the first time since I arrived, Laura smiled.

"This one was taken at Crystal Beach near the amusement park. That was a new bathing suit, I remember. It was peach. I tried my first cigarette that day and hated it. I crushed it in the sand after two puffs and your father got angry because of the rationing."

She flipped to another picture, the one in front of the fountain. "I forget the name of this hotel. It will come to me. We were there for a wedding. The groom was killed a year later in the war."

Her smile was broadest when she saw the picture of herself at the lunch counter. "Your father always wanted me to pull my skirt higher."

"You can keep those," I said. "He'd want you to have them."

She handed back the photographs. "I have my own."

I placed the pictures back in the humidor. Sunlight reflected off the engagement ring and I kept the lid open.

"So," Laura said, "You drove all this way to find out about me."

"It was on my way home."

She rocked and nodded. "Albany is close, isn't it? All these years we were so close."

"You knew that I lived there?"

"I know all about Albany."

It was my turn to rock and think this over. After a minute, I reached into the humidor and handed her the engagement ring. Her hand shook as she held it.

"He kept it," she whispered.

"I found it in his things."

She closed the ring in her fist and looked down Union Avenue. "My maiden name was Sanders," she said. "Does that sound familiar?"

"A Mr. Sanders owned the building our restaurant was in. I only saw him a few times. He didn't come down very often, but I remember my father and grandfather whispering about him. They'd always stop talking when I entered the room. We didn't buy the building until after he died."

Laura faced me. "That was Louis Sanders, my father. He owned that whole block. He sold off the buildings one at a time over the years, but not yours. He held onto that until he died. It didn't matter what your grandfather or father offered him, he would always turn them down. I'm the one who finally sold it to your father when I settled the estate."

"Why wouldn't he sell?"

Laura leaned back in the chair and shut her eyes, as if she were visualizing it all again. "When your father came home from the war, I became pregnant. It didn't matter to your father, since we were going to be married anyway." She opened her eyes and then her hand and looked down at the engagement ring. "That's all we talked about. It was in every letter we sent each other when he was overseas. Us getting married."

"You were pregnant?" I asked, trying hard but failing at imagining my father in that situation. "Why didn't he marry you?"

"A Sanders doesn't marry beneath them, according to my father. I can still hear him—'You want to marry the *dishwasher*? Have his greasy bastard?'" She shook her head. "We were going to elope to Niagara Falls, but somehow my father found out. He swore that if I married Gus, he'd shut the restaurant down and evict your family. They were still living above the restaurant then—your grandparents and father—and he said he'd throw them out in the street. He would have done it, too. I couldn't let that happen. They had barely survived the Depression without losing everything and couldn't afford to start over, not then. I didn't know what would happen to them, so I gave the ring to George and my father took me here."

"You left without talking to Dad?"

"It was part of the deal I made with my father. It was to protect the restaurant, your family."

"Did my father know all this?" I asked, my voice rising in disbelief. I was getting a story I hadn't expected and one, I was sure, I hadn't wanted.

"Not for years. He hated me for a long time."

"Your daughter, the woman I spoke to on the phone, is she my...?"

Laura shook her head. "The baby was taken care of by a doctor, a friend of the family. Father arranged the abortion."

"When did my father find all this out?"

Her irises darkened to a deeper gray, all traces of the yellow specs disappearing. "The summer you turned twelve."

"That's an odd way to remember it," I said, shifting in the rocking chair, gripped by a strange feeling that maybe Uncle George was right, that I should've just left it alone.

"The winter before that my husband died in a car accident. In the summer, I reached out to your father. Between what my father and husband had left me, I was suddenly a very wealthy woman."

"He wouldn't leave."

"He wouldn't leave *you*. You were twelve," she said, her voice gathering strength like a growing storm. "He said a boy needed his father at that age. So we made plans for when you graduated high school and could take over the restaurant. Then he'd be free, he said. You could run it and take care of your mother. We'd send money back to help."

I couldn't look at her and stared at the blanket on her lap. "But I went to college."

"In *Albany*," she said, spitting the word out like a bite of spoiled fruit. "Three hundred miles away. You promised you'd study business and then come back and run the restaurant, remember? Do you remember your promise?"

There was a rushing in my ears when I nodded.

"Then you wanted an MBA. You told him you had big plans for the restaurant. How you were going to change everything, go upscale, make it so you wouldn't have to struggle so much and not just scrape by like he and your grandfather had. You told him you were learning so much. And you kept promising to come back and run things."

I stared at the porch floor, remembering all those promises, all those conversations with my father, all those times he had asked me when I was coming home.

"Then you met a nice Albany girl. Her father owned a plastics company, didn't he? You're still doing well there?"

"He said he was proud of me," I said, my voice as weak as Uncle George's.

"What else could he say?"

"I never knew any of this," I whispered. "He never said a word."

"He didn't think he had to. He thought you'd keep your promise. He'd never leave your mother alone and when she was diagnosed with

Parkinson's, he could never leave her at all. Then it was just too damn late for us."

I sat statue still in that chair, but the feeling of motion, of perpetual rocking, overcame me. I could see my father's face from years ago and his melancholy eyes, the eyes I'd inherited. He was looking at me, through me, his stare revealing so much now.

A car parked in front of the house then, and a woman got out. I watched her open the trunk and pull out a grocery bag as I gripped the arms of the rocking chair, trying to stop everything from moving so fast and hoping my father's face would disappear.

Laura handed me the ring, her voice low, bitter. "I needed this when you were twelve and then when you were eighteen. I needed this when you were twenty-two and then when you turned twenty-four. Not *now*."

I closed my fingers around the ring. It felt like I was holding an ejected shell casing, still hot from being fired.

"You must be Chris," the woman holding the grocery bag said, smiling and walking toward us. "I'm Joyce. We talked on the phone."

Then I was on my feet, the front porch pitching beneath me, mumbling hello, shaking her hand, trying to return her smile.

"Did you have a nice visit?" she asked, turning toward her mother. "Did you remember his father?"

"We had a good talk," Laura answered with a sharp nod and leaned far back in her chair. "Long overdue."

I looked at the Bulova and then heard myself say how I had to get going, that I had a wife who was waiting for me, how she'd made me promise to come home early.

Laura rocked harder, the blanket slipping off her lap, but said nothing.

"Albany isn't far," Joyce said. "You'll have to come back and tell me about your father some time."

I told her I would but knew I wouldn't keep that promise, either; Laura knew it, too. I returned the ring to the humidor and shut the lid. I don't remember walking down the porch steps or crossing the front lawn to my car. I was halfway down Union Avenue when I had to pull to the curb, the road swimming before me, blurring and undulating like I had been drinking all afternoon. I rolled my window down and felt the cool air on my face, the temperature dropping with the descending sun.

A motorcycle roared past my parked car with its headers wide open. A girl with auburn hair spilling from her helmet clung to the biker, her arms wrapped around him like she'd never let go. I thought of James Junior then, and how he had raced up and down High Street the night of my father's funeral, trying to outrun whatever he'd buried inside himself. I thought of my mother, too—had she known about Laura and my father but married him anyway, silently knowing he loved her far less? Of course I thought of my father and all that he had carried, all that had eluded him, and could only imagine what he'd thought of me and the promises I'd broken. And then I thought of Jenny and everything we had locked away from each other, and I wondered if it would ever be possible to open those boxes, to bring out those mementos, to see if they would stand or wither in the unrelenting light.

The Girl in the Window

Originally published in *Echo Ink Review*

Carlton first saw the girl in the window on a July night when the air was so heavy and still, it felt as if no one in the neighborhood were breathing. She was leaning out of a second-floor window of a Lexington Avenue flat. A cigarette burned between her fingers, and he waited for her to raise it to her lips, to inhale deeply, to shoot twin streams of smoke through her nostrils and into the darkness, but she never did.

Her profile was turned toward where he leaned against a tree, swallowed in shadows and shielded from the streetlight. He took in her straight Roman nose and how she wore her hair up and off her neck on that hot summer night; her black curls were swirled and pinned to the top of her head, a few wisps dangling free. She wore a white tank-top, her breasts full and rounded against the material, and Carlton felt desire vibrate through his body. He guessed her to be about his age, late twenties, and he wondered if she were alone but then pushed that thought away, certain a woman that beautiful could never be alone. He waited for a man to come from behind and place a hand on her shoulder, to kiss the top of her head, to slowly rub an ice cube across her neck, along her clavicle, between her breasts. No one appeared.

Then Carlton did something he had never done on all those nights he had volunteered for Neighborhood Watch Patrol and had hidden in the darkness and peered through windows. He placed a cigarette between his lips and announced himself with a flick of his lighter, his face briefly illuminated by the flame. The girl in the window turned and stared at his cigarette's red glow. Carlton inhaled fully, making the tip burn brighter. His hand shook as he waited for her to shout at him, or to yell for her man who must be somewhere in that apartment, or to reach for her cell phone to call the police about the voyeur, but she didn't move. She only stared, her face unreadable.

He was almost done with his smoke when the girl looked away and flicked her own cigarette out the window; it hit the empty driveway in sparks. Turning back to him, she stared in his direction and then rose. Carlton sighed, the sound almost a moan, when he saw she was wearing only the tank-top and panties. She paused, reached for the light switch, and then she, too, was lost in darkness.

Carlton's hand still shook as he pulled the notebook from his back pocket, the notebook in which he was supposed to write down license plate numbers and descriptions of suspicious characters. He glanced at his military watch with glowing tritium hands and entered the time and her address.

The image of the girl in the window stayed with Carlton all the next day. While performing mundane tasks—folding laundry, making his bed quarter-bouncing tight, shaving—the girl in the window would rise before him like heat shimmering off the desert floor. He would again see her profile, the swell of her breasts, the smoothness of her thighs, and his mouth would grow sand dry. As he filled out the police officer application at City Hall, he imagined coming to her from behind and burying his face in her piled curls, breathing her in, and feeling the July heat on her arms as he caressed her from shoulder to wrist and then up again. Carlton could feel her lean into him, the back of her head against his chest like an undeserved gift.

He looked down at the half-completed application, trying to focus, but the questions—Years of Active Duty, Date of Honorable Discharge, Medals and Citations Awarded—swirled into unreadable black pools.

~

He arrived at her flat at the same time the second night, so anxious to see her again that he had skipped patrolling the playground on St. James Street. Her window was dark, and the deep disappointment startled him. He shut his eyes, willing his heart and lungs to slow, his pulse to grow faint, the way he tried when the memories flooded back of looking through the exploded window of that Iraqi home and the six dead Marines blown, literally, to pieces inside the small stone house. He had stood in that window for what seemed like a lifetime, trying to figure out what happened and why. Then he felt a tap on the shoulder and heard the order to go on casualty collection—putting the pieces in body bags. His hands and arms had felt slick by the time he was done.

When Carlton opened his eyes, the girl was framed in the lighted window wearing a halter-top the color of dollar bills. She rested her chin in her palm and gazed towards the tree; he wondered if she could see him. Carlton felt something inside him soar, and he stepped forward, stopping just before coming completely into view. The girl in the window raised her head slightly at the movement from the shadows, and Carlton thought that just for an instant, she looked pleased. With two fingers he fished a cigarette from his shirt pocket, and after he lit it, he didn't extinguish the lighter. His features flickered with the flame, and after he was certain she had seen him, he doused the dancing light. Her expression didn't change. The corners of her mouth didn't curl into a smile. She looked away.

Carlton smoked the cigarette slowly, taking long drags, the tip a beacon. His gaze never broke from the window. When he had ashed it almost to the filter, he flicked the butt in an arc as she had done the previous night. She watched it smolder in her empty driveway and then turned to the tree. Carlton thought of moving into the streetlight's murky circle, but his boots were leaden, his legs unresponsive. He was too far away to tell the color of her eyes. They must be dark like her hair, brown or black, and he wished they had unearthly powers that would lock him in powerful beams and pull him into view, but they were just eyes.

Without acknowledging that he even existed, the girl in the window reached behind her neck and untied her halter-top, letting it fall free. Carlton's pounding heartbeat measured the time that passed before she stood and reached for the light switch, leaving him wanting. He waited before leaving the tree's shadow, certain she was watching him from her darkened room as he walked away, his legs trembling.

He didn't try to sleep that night; sleep never came easily anyway, if it ever came at all. They didn't tell him about that during the Exit Counseling and Reintegration session or how it would feel unnatural to sleep in a bed after sleeping on the ground for so long; they didn't tell him about the nightmares. So that night he kept patrolling, walking past the boundaries of his neighborhood and up and down unfamiliar streets until the sky paled to the color of a fresh bruise. By daybreak, he had retrieved his car and was parked across the street from the girl's apartment. Lexington Avenue woke around him as families began pulling out of driveways and runners and cyclists hurried past in pairs. In the trees, cicadas called to each other, announcing that another sultry day was in store.

At 7:20, the girl in the window walked down her driveway and turned toward Elmwood Avenue. She wore a navy pencil-skirt and a white short-sleeved blouse. A small black purse was slung over her shoulder. Her hair was still piled up but neater now, every strand pinned and sprayed. Large, dark sunglasses covered her face. Carlton thought she looked like a movie star. At the corner, she crossed at the light and waited for the southbound bus toward downtown.

He scrambled out of his car and hurried to the corner. He didn't know what time the bus came—he didn't patrol in the morning—and almost jogged to Elmwood, fearing he would miss it. Sweat trickled down his sides, and his shirt began to stick to his back, but he had been in hotter places and hardly noticed.

They stood on opposite corners as he waited for the light to change. She was looking north, the direction the bus would arrive from, and he was watching her come in and out of view between gaps in flowing traffic. When the light turned green, he crossed the street, his heart thudding like an artillery barrage. He was certain she'd see it pounding through his golf shirt exactly where 'Patrol' was embossed above the breast pocket. She glanced at him briefly and turned toward the Number 20 bus belching exhaust as it approached. Carlton had just reached the curb when the bus pulled in front of the stop, its air brakes releasing like a held breath.

She took a seat by the window in the middle of the bus, as he dug in his pockets for the fare. The driver jerked the bus in gear, and Carlton had to steady himself against the seats while making his way down the aisle. The girl continued looking out the window at the usual morning sights—a produce delivery at the Co-Op, the steady stream of people in and out of Spot Coffee, the panhandlers already on the corners. She didn't turn toward him when he took a seat two rows back and across the aisle from her.

He had hoped for a smile or for her to move her purse from the seat next to her as an invitation. He thought there would be some recognition, some type of acknowledgment, but she only stared out the window. Maybe the distance from her bedroom to the tree was too great, and she hadn't seen his face clearly in the lighter's weak glow last evening. Or maybe she had. Suddenly, he felt tired.

The bus rattled and bounced down Elmwood Avenue, and Carlton studied the back of her head, her slender neck, the occasional glimpse of her profile, but she never turned around. If she sensed his staring, she didn't show it. As they approached the corner of South Elmwood and Court Street, she raised her tanned arm and pulled the bell cord for the driver to stop. Carlton watched her make her way up the aisle, his eyes on her skirted hips and the curve of her calves. She stopped and turned. Looking directly at him she said, "I'll be on Lexington Avenue at midnight. Find me," then stepped through the bus doors.

Carlton straightened in his seat as if those nine words had grabbed him by the collar and raised him almost to standing. She had spoken so suddenly and quickly, he wondered if he'd imagined it. He heard the blood thrum in his ears and grow louder, more distinct, metastasizing throughout his body and amplifying until he was sure those sitting around him could hear it. He watched as the girl crossed in front of the bus and headed toward the office building with mirrored windows, and wondered what she'd meant. There was one bar on Lexington Avenue, The Place. Maybe she would be there, waiting for him.

As the bus lurched from the corner, Carlton tried to imagine her in the office break-room, coffee cup in hand, telling her co-workers about the man outside her window and how she would meet him that night, but he couldn't bring that image into focus.

At midnight, Carlton was patrolling Lexington Avenue, walking in the same direction he did every night. He was three blocks from the girl's house, The Place's neon sign still a green glow in the distance, when he heard breaking glass. Without hesitating, he began running toward the noise, carrying his heavy police flashlight like a sprinter's baton, his combat boots thudding on the sidewalk with each stride. In one fluid motion, his walkie-talkie was off his hip and at his mouth. He called in his position, where he was headed, and what he had heard. He slowed when he saw her standing in the moonlight by a parked car, a ball-peen hammer in her hand. The car was old, rusted in spots, primed in others, missing hubcaps. The front passenger side window, the one closest to her, was partially shattered.

She stood looking in his direction, her body still. Her face and arms glistened with perspiration, the night providing little respite from the heat. She was breathing deep and fast, her chest heaving in the white tank-top she had worn the first night he'd seen her. He stopped a few feet from her. It was the closest they'd ever been; the sound of their breathing blended in an evening duet. He looked from her to the shattered car window and saw a large, beige purse sitting on the passenger seat, carelessly forgotten by its owner. Turning back to her, he didn't see fear in her eyes, only a mix of anticipation and curiosity as to what he'd do next. The corners of her mouth turned slightly upward as she raised her chin, daring him.

The Patrol Coordinator's voice crackled from the walkie-talkie, breaking through the static, wanting to know where he was, what he saw, telling him the police were on their way. The girl dropped her glance to the radio, and when she raised her eyes, they seemed wider, darker, consisting entirely of pupil and asking, *What now?*

In that instant, Carlton thought of all the patrols he had been on and how he'd left a little part of himself behind on each one, losing that part forever in blowing and shifting sands. And he thought of that other window and how he'd left the biggest and best parts of himself inside that blasted house. But he mostly thought how the girl standing in front of him now looked so beautiful, so alive, so real.

As he swung his flashlight, a siren wailed in the distance. More glass shattered as he widened the broken window opening. The girl shifted her weight from one tanned leg to the other. As he reached for the purse, a jagged shard sliced his arm from wrist to elbow, leaving a painful red gash that he knew would scar.

Originally anthologized in the *Best Short Stories from the Saturday Evening Post Great American Fiction Contest 2013*

The Wolf Boy disappeared from Forest Lawn Cemetery on the day I moved into my new apartment. The radio in the kitchen was playing, so I learned the news from a muffled voice coming from a distant room as I unpacked. Jason Wolf and his sixth grade class from the City Honors School were visiting the cemetery as the conclusion to their year-long study of local history. Somewhere between Chief Red Jacket's monument and President Millard Fillmore's grave, the teachers noticed that Jason was missing. They assumed the boy had wandered off but would soon be found.

They were wrong.

The police were notified and squad cars crept up and down the cemetery's curved and intertwined roadways, the cops calling his name through loudspeakers. By the time I ate my dinner that night in front of the television and surrounded by empty boxes, all the local channels were broadcasting live from the cemetery about Jason's disappearance. His class picture was shown, along with a phone number to call if anyone had seen a ginger-haired boy wearing khaki shorts and a white golf shirt in the vicinity of Forest Lawn.

By morning, volunteers from Jason's school crisscrossed the grounds on foot, moving in a grid, finding nothing.

Searching the cemetery was no easy task.

Forest Lawn was inspired by the designers of Paris' *Père-Lachais*, who believed a cemetery should be a celebration of not only lives already lived, but the life that continues after us, and represented by a lush, natural, rugged setting. The cemetery consisted of 269 acres of rolling hills and valleys, spring-fed lakes, twisting creeks, and ten thousand trees. It also backed up to Delaware Park with its additional 350 acres of meadow, forest, and lake.

The Wolf Boy's story interested me because Jason was a middle schooler, and I had just been hired to teach English at PS 64, the public middle school in the same neighborhood as Jason's school for gifted children. I was to begin that September, and it would be my first teaching job out of college. Jason could've been my student, lost on my watch during a class field trip. Some of my incoming students in the fall may have known him from the neighborhood, or gone to elementary school with him, or at least seen him around.

Over those next few days after his disappearance, however, we all got to know the Wolf Boy from the news reports: how he was an excellent student, an only child, and had visited the emergency room several times over the years for suspicious bumps, bruises and, once, a broken wrist. We learned how the police had been summoned to his home twice this past year on domestic disturbance calls. Another picture emerged as well: how he was a Scout and loved to hike, fish, and camp. Interviewed neighbors told how his tent was always set up in the backyard, and how he would sleep in it even in foul weather. It made me wonder how bad life inside his home must have been if he always wanted to stay outside in a potentially leaky tent. As the days passed and he was still not found, we were told how family and friends clung to the hope that his outdoor skills would help him survive until rescuers found him. But he wasn't found, no ransom note was received, and each day the Wolf Boy was in the news less and less.

By September, I had nearly forgotten about him. I had my own problems to worry about. Because of a maternity leave, a nervous breakdown, and an unfortunate late-summer lawn mowing accident, PS 64's Science Department was down three teachers. I was told that I, an English teacher, would not only be teaching seventh grade Science for the first semester, but I'd also be in charge of the seventh grade Fall

Expedition, a semester-long study of a topic explored in-depth from the perspective of as many classes as possible—History, Art, Geography, Science, Math, and Music. In past years students explored the development of the city, the impact of immigration, and our natural waterways. The year the Wolf Boy disappeared, our expedition focused on Forest Lawn Cemetery and Delaware Park.

Two days before school started, I sat in my classroom learning about native plant life. I heard a knock on my open door and glanced up to see a woman standing in my doorway. She gave me a small, tentative smile, revealing a space between her top front teeth that I found endearing.

"Are you busy?"

"No, not at all," I said, standing and moving toward her. "I was just reading about *eleocharis tortilis*."

She bit her lip as she thought. "Wright's Spikerush?"

"*Twisted* Spikerush," I corrected. "If these notes are right."

"I'm Pat Green," she said, extending her hand. "The long-term sub for Mr. Clark."

I squinted at her. "Clark? Lawn mower accident teacher?"

"No, nervous breakdown teacher."

"I'm David," I said, shaking her hand. "Maternity leave replacement teacher."

She was petite with flashing dark eyes and high, delicate cheekbones. A yellow short-sleeved blouse clung to her, and I guessed her to be ten years older than I, maybe more. I glanced at her tanned left hand and noticed the pale line where she had recently worn a wedding ring. It was difficult not to stare.

She walked in and glanced around my bare science lab. The only things that hung on the walls were a clock that ran twelve minutes fast and, strangely, a portrait of John F. Kennedy, as if he were still the sitting president.

"I love what you've done with the place," she said.

"I haven't had a chance to work on my bulletin board or hang posters. I'm trying to figure out how to teach Science."

She flashed her gapped smile. "Me, too."

"Have you been teaching long?"

"I'm trying to get back into it," she answered, looking out on the student lab tables, as if she were picturing the seats filled with seventh graders. "I'm hoping this will turn into a full-time position."

"That would be great."

She turned to me, her dark eyes looking nervous and shifting, their gaze moving around my bare room until they settled on me. "I wanted to talk to you about Cole."

"Cole?"

"My son. He'll be in your first-period class. He should be on your roster."

I glanced at the rosters sitting untouched on my desk. "Yes, of course."

She nodded. "I wanted to ask you for a favor. Well, two favors, actually."

"Sure. Anything."

She bit her lip again before she spoke, this time harder, so the color drained. "Cole is a good kid. A smart kid, really. But he has a hard time focusing and is easily distracted."

"A lot of boys have that problem in middle school," I said, trying to remember if this were true. It sounded right.

"He was in trouble a lot last year because of being disruptive or just not engaging at all."

"I see," I said, nodding and furrowing my brows, attempting to look like a teacher.

"I'm worried how he'll be this year. My husband and I separated over the summer and Cole is going through a hard time. I'm afraid he'll be even more of a problem this semester."

So she was available.

"Which brings me to the first favor," she said, taking a deep breath. "I don't want you to treat him differently than any other student. I'm not looking for special treatment."

"Of course not," I said, watching her pulse flutter in the soft, kissable hollow of her throat.

"But if his behavior gets out of hand, if things have to be elevated, could you just let me know before you report him?"

"Absolutely," I said, forcing my eyes to stay locked on hers and not drift downward. "That's not a problem at all."

"Maybe if I know beforehand I can talk to him, try to get him to straighten up before the administrators are involved."

'Sure," I said. "I want what's best for Cole, too."

Her whole body relaxed then, and her smile was wide. "Thank you."

"No problem," I said, like I was accustomed to solving student problems. "What kind of kid is he? What's he into? Sports? Music?"

Her body once again tensed as if a key had been inserted. "Jason Wolf."

"What about him?"

"That's what he's into. Jason Wolf. He's become obsessed with him ever since his disappearance. He cuts out articles about him and hangs them in his room. He draws pictures of him in the woods, living in a cave and fishing."

"Why?"

"They were in Scouts together until Cole decided scouting was stupid and dropped out. Jason was always the top scout. The newspaper's right; he is a regular Daniel Boone. He had more merit badges than anybody. Cole is convinced that Jason is alive, that he planned the whole thing and is living in the park and cemetery like some savage. And right now, unfortunately, the idea of living in the woods, away from his family situation, is very attractive to Cole."

"Are you afraid he might sneak off to the cemetery? To try to be with the Wolf...with Jason?"

Her chin quivered as she nodded.

"I'm sorry, Pat," I said, reaching out to lay a consoling hand, briefly, upon her warm arm, her arm so richly tanned I imagined her massaging coconut-scented creams and lotions into her skin until it glistened in the summer sun.

She took a deep breath, recomposing herself, before she continued. "My second favor is if I could co-chair the science part of the expedition with you. If I'm involved in all the planning, if I know what's to take place and when, if I'm there as a chaperone to keep an eye on him, it would make me feel as if I'm in control somehow."

"Sure. Absolutely," I said, imagining us working closely together and getting to know each other.

"Thank you," she said.

I looked at the clock running twelve minutes fast. "It's getting late. Do you want to go for coffee or a drink and figure out the Expedition? I have the folder Mrs. Durant started that we could go through," I said, and half-turned, pointing to a stack of folders on my desk. I was almost certain I saw an Expedition folder in the pile.

She hesitated for a moment, weighing the pros and the cons, the implications, the messages, real or perceived, which were being sent, and then, finally, declined.

My students were confused on the first day of school. One after another or in pairs, they walked through my door, took two steps into the classroom, then stopped when they saw my posters of Dickens and Steinbeck hanging on the wall, the bust of Hemingway on the lab table in front of the room, and my 'Read Banned Books' bulletin board. They looked down at their class schedules, checked the room number, and then looked up at me with uncertainty and a touch of fear splashed across their faces.

"Come in," I said. "You're in the right room if you have Science this period. I'm Mr. Sanders."

"What's with all the stupid book posters then?" one boy asked, slouching his way to an open desk. His wore his hair long and it hung in his eyes; he'd flick his head, tossing his hair aside so he could see. Even if Pat hadn't showed me the photo she carried in her wallet, I would have recognized her son right away. They shared the same dark, almond-shaped eyes and high cheekbones. He was a sullen version of her.

"Those posters will be replaced with more science-oriented ones as the semester goes on. I just wanted to have something on the walls for now."

"Weird," Cole muttered as he slid into his seat and began immediately to draw.

As more of my students filed into the classroom and filled the empty desks, the more I found myself pacing in front of the lab table, a manic energy coursing through me as I greeted them. I'm sure I would have been nervous on my very first day of teaching no matter what, but my anxiety was compounded by not only being forced to teach an unfamiliar subject, but also by having Cole in my class. Pat and I had stayed late twice to plan the Expedition, and each time I'd asked if she'd like to get a drink or a bite to eat afterwards. Each time she had politely refused. I had a feeling that if I were going to get anywhere with her, Cole would be the key. I wanted all my students to like me, to think I was the cool new teacher, but especially Cole. I was certain that if I could win him over, I'd win over Pat as well.

After the bell rang to signal the start of class, the majority of the period was spent doing housekeeping tasks: reviewing homework, attendance, and detention policies; explaining the grading system for the semester; and handing out lab books. Cole ignored me the entire time, his head bent to his drawing. Occasionally, I would hear him sigh or mutter "boring" under his breath.

"The real foundation for the fall semester is the seventh grade Expedition. Does anyone know what that is?" I asked, looking out on rows of blank, bored faces.

I looked toward Cole, but his head was resting on the crook of his arm. Pat had told me she wasn't going to tell him about the trip until she had to; she was afraid he'd start making plans like Jason had.

"Don't we go somewhere and study something?" a girl in the front row answered. I think her name was Jill. Or Judy.

"That's right," I said. "And this year, all the seventh graders—not just this class, the whole seventh grade—will go camping in Delaware Park and Forest Lawn to study the wildlife and plant life of the region. It will give you a feel how real biologists and botanists work in the field and the skills and tools they use to conduct research."

Cole's head snapped up. "The cemetery?"

Jill-Judy wrinkled her nose. "We're going to camp out on *graves*?"

"No, we'll camp in the park, but we'll spend a lot of time studying the flora of the cemetery. They named it Forest Lawn for a reason, right?"

"The Wolf Boy lives in the cemetery," Cole said.

Jill-Judy half-turned in her seat and looked back at Cole. "No, he doesn't. He disappeared *from* the cemetery. He doesn't *live* there."

"Yeah, he does," Cole answered. "He's like Mega Scout. He could live anywhere."

"I heard that, too," another boy with a mouthful of silver braces said. "He's a jungle boy."

"I think he's part Indian," a girl with acne said. "Iroquois or something."

"He is not. I went to Sunday School with him," a red-headed kid said. "I think he's German."

Suddenly my class was alive. For the first time that morning, they were attentive, engaged, and talking. I'd lit upon a topic that interested them—the Wolf Boy—and everybody had an opinion.

"Why couldn't the police find him in the cemetery then?"

"Because he's the Wolf Boy!" Cole yelled.

"Some psycho got him. They'll find his chopped up and rotted body next spring when the snow melts."

"Gross."

"Yeah, and what about the snow? How's he going to survive the winter?"

"I heard he runs around the cemetery naked," a kid in the back of the room said.

"You're weird," the girl next to him said.

"What does he eat?" Jill-Judy asked.

Suddenly I saw how I could reach them, how I might actually educate them. "Okay, okay. Time out," I said, making a 'T' with my hands like a referee. "Jill raises a good question."

"Judy," she corrected.

"Judy," I repeated, and smiled apologetically before walking towards the chalkboard. "What *would* the Wolf Boy eat if he were living in Delaware Park and Forest Lawn?"

No one answered.

"Come on," I said, the chalk poised above the board, my heart beating fast. "What would he eat? Call them out."

"Plants?" Judy asked.

"Absolutely," I said, writing it down.

"Nuts," someone else called.

I added it to the list.

"Berries."

"Fish."

"Squirrels."

"There's deer in the park."

"How's he going to kill a deer?"

"He's the Wolf Boy," Cole said. "He can do anything."

"There's lots of birds there."

"Ducks."

"Geese."

"Rabbits."

"I saw a turtle there once."

"He could set out buckets and drink rain water."

"Where's he going to get a bucket?"

"He could kill the deer with the bucket. Just sneak up on it and smack it in the head."

"Moron."

I turned to face them. "Okay, settle down," I said, and miraculously they quieted. I jerked my thumb over my shoulder. "That's a pretty good list you came up with, and you came up with it fast. And guess what? That's what we're going to study during the expedition. We're going to study the plants and animals of the park. We'll identify and name them. Categorize them by their species and scientific names. The *specific* plants. The *specific* berries. The *specific* nuts. The types of birds that live there. What *would* the Wolf Boy eat? What plants would make him sick? Which flowers are edible?"

For the first time all period, Cole raised his hand, his eyes bright, his face flushed. "You mean the whole semester is going to be about the Wolf Boy?"

The bell rang like an alarm, signaling the end of class. "Yes," I said, words rushing from my mouth before I had a chance to stop them. "This whole semester is going to be about the Wolf Boy."

I was sitting at my kitchen table that night, trying to learn the next day's lesson plans, when the phone rang. Pat's voice was low and angry on the other end of the receiver. "This semester is *not* about Jason," she said, and I imagined her spitting the words through the adorable space between her teeth. "How could you *say* that?"

"I reached them, Pat! All of them, but especially Cole."

"This is *not* what we talked about. This is *not* what we planned."

"I know, but they got excited. They got excited about learning. They got excited about *trees*. Wasn't Cole excited?"

There was a pause on the line before Pat admitted, "It's all he's been talking about since he got home."

"See? When's the last time he's been this eager to learn?"

"Never," she said, her voice still low but the anger now drained from it.

"I think I'm on to something with this Wolf Boy angle, Pat. I really do. I think it will work. Why don't we meet for a beer and brainstorm about it?"

She hung up without saying goodbye.

The next several weeks were spent preparing for our excursion to the park and cemetery. In History, they learned about Fredrick Law Olmsted, the designer of Delaware Park, and his other work around the city as well as the lives of those buried in Forest Lawn—Chief Red Jacket, President Fillmore, Civil War General Daniel Bidwell, and the nineteenth century industrialists who brought the city into its golden age. In Art, the students learned sketching techniques and studied the artists— Charles Cary Rumsey, Grace Goodyear, Antonio Ugo—whose bronze sculptures are found in the cemetery. In Health class they learned emergency first aid; survival techniques; and identifying poison ivy, oak, and sumac.

In my class, they learned about the Wolf Boy.

I broke my students into teams. One group researched which plants the Wolf Boy could eat and how to identify them. Another group reported on the poisonous ones he had to avoid. A third group cataloged the fauna and ranked them from the easiest to hardest to catch. Cole led the team studying the cemetery's and park's physical layouts. He poured over maps like Eisenhower planning D-Day—he found aerial photographs; he studied Olmsted's original design; he identified areas where the Wolf Boy most likely lived.

"Heavily wooded to avoid detection and close to a water supply," he told us when he presented his findings to the class, pointing to the map he'd hung on the wall, replacing my Steinbeck poster. From the moment he'd heard that the whole semester was going to be about the Wolf Boy, Cole had become my best student. He gave his presentation without reading from his notes, and he referenced the artwork and monuments he'd learned about in his other classes. He knew more about Delaware Park and Forest Lawn than anybody.

Pat stood in the doorway watching, fear and pride alternating across her pretty face. Cole's presentation ran long, right up until the bell rang, and the other students clapped when he finished. When Cole passed me to head to his next class, he gave me a high five, slapping my hand hard.

After the last student hurried out, I turned to Pat, smiling. "He was good, wasn't he? It was the best presentation so far."

"Congratulations," she said, her eyes as black and hard as stones. "You've turned my son into the Wolf Boy."

She left my classroom before I could answer, her heels clicking down the hallway like low-caliber gunfire.

The Expedition took place over Columbus Day Weekend that year. The temperature was still warm enough that we could wear shorts during the day and hold off donning sweatshirts or light jackets until early evening when the air turned crisp, foreshadowing the colder, darker hours ahead. The foliage was near peak. Oaks and elms were ablaze with color, and fallen acorns crunched under our feet as we hiked to our campsite. The kids kicked chestnuts at each other.

"There are a ton of these," a voice behind me said.

"*Castanea dentata*," another voice said.

"He could roast them," the first student answered. "He could eat these all winter."

I smiled.

They had learned something.

I had taught them.

"Don't look so damned pleased with yourself," Pat said in a low voice, hiking beside me. Cole was about ten feet ahead of us on the path; Pat never took her eyes off him.

"He'll be fine, Pat. All the chaperones know the situation. Everyone's keeping an eye on him."

"You don't know anything. When you're a parent you'll understand. Christ, you're just a kid yourself," she said, and she hurried away from me to catch up with her son, her words stinging, my eyes never leaving her calves.

Cole disappeared the second night of the expedition.

He'd snuck off with his sleeping bag and backpack sometime after lights-out, not disturbing anyone. I imagined him dressed in black, creeping past chaperones who were supposed to be vigilant, his mother who swore she wouldn't sleep the entire trip, and rows of tents containing his slumbering classmates.

The news spread quickly through the camp. Students huddled together in front of their tents as the soft morning light of autumn fell upon them. Some cried, others looked scared. A few wore dazed expressions, bordering on awe.

"He did it. He actually *did* it," Jeremy, the boy with braces, said, as if Cole had shared his plan ahead of time.

Pat came up to me, hate and fear in her dark eyes, tears streaming down her pretty face. She punched me hard on the chest with the side of her fist, like she was hammering a spike through my heart. "I *told* you this would happen."

"We'll find him, Pat," I said, trying to keep my voice from trembling. "He's not gone."

"He's not? Then where the fuck is he, David?"

Panic gripped me; I'd never thought Cole would sneak away. He'd seemed so happy these last few weeks, so engaged, a different boy from the one who had slouched into my classroom six weeks earlier. Everyone—Pat, the students, the other chaperones—stared, waiting for me to answer Pat's question, waiting for me to take charge, waiting for me to teach.

"The rugged part of the cemetery," I said, pointing toward Forest Lawn, the idea just coming to me but certain I was right. "On that ridge where it's all overgrown. That's where he'll look for the Wolf Boy first."

"How do you know?" Pat asked.

"He told us in his presentation. Heavily wooded and close to water, remember? The stream runs right through there. That's the closest spot that's like that."

"You're just guessing."

"If he's not there, we'll try the next rugged spot and then the next and work our way to the woods, following the stream. That's what he'll do. He's trying to find the Wolf Boy, Pat. I'm certain of it."

"Goddamn you, David."

"We need to go *now*," I said, and she and the others believed me.

We didn't break camp; the tents were left standing in the park. The students were mobilized, eating granola bars and drinking juice pouches as we marched toward the cemetery. I told them not to call out Cole's name, as that would make him hide from us, but occasionally a student would yell for him, or howl like a wolf, or get excited and point out a Red-tailed hawk—"*Buteo jamaicensis!*"—and Pat would snap at them to be quiet.

We marched among headstones dating back to the 1830s, their inscriptions worn by time and weather. We circled Mirror Lake and passed the Birge Memorial, a massive monument supported by twelve Doric columns and with the president of the old Pierce Arrow Motor Car Company buried beneath the marble.

I kept my eyes on the rough ridge on the other side of the lake, periodically raising my binoculars and scanning the tree line for movement, spotting nothing but a doe on the move, doing her best to avoid the young bucks during rutting season. My hands shook as I held the binoculars.

We fanned into a line of students and chaperones as we ascended the hill, the ground becoming steeper and rockier with each step. My plan was to march to the stream maintaining that line, trapping Cole between us and the water's edge. As we moved forward, I looked for some sign that he had been there—a discarded candy wrapper, an apple core, some piece of the life he was trying to leave behind. Then I found myself looking for some sign of the Wolf Boy—a smoldering campfire, the gutted remains of a small animal, remnants of shed clothing. I saw none of these things, and a dizzying fear touched me deep to the marrow that maybe both boys really were gone.

Then we heard the scream.

Raw. Primal. Like a howl. The sound froze us. Pat's eyes locked on mine, growing wider as the shriek continued. She mouthed Cole's name, somehow recognizing it as her son's wail. It sounded like he was in agony.

When the screaming stopped, we moved towards where we thought the sound had come. Then the wailing began again, the throat-ripping sound guiding us. We stumbled over rocks and roots, our feet slipping on loose stones and dirt, as we headed towards the fading cry.

We found Cole at the base of a rocky embankment on his knees, his arms wrapped around himself, his upper body rocking. He was kneeling three feet from the Wolf Boy. Pat slid down to him and threw her arms around his shoulders, trying to turn her son away from the corpse.

It didn't take a biologist or a coroner or even a science teacher to see that Jason had been dead a long time. The elements and animals had left too much evidence to dispute that. We'd later learn from the local paper that he had died soon after his disappearance, that he had lost his footing, toppled down the hill, and struck his ginger-haired head on a rock, dying instantly. Authorities speculated that he had evaded them until the search had been called off. There'd been no campfires, no living off the land, no months of survival on his own.

There'd been no Wolf Boy.

There'd only been Jason Wolf, an eleven-year-old boy who'd grow no older.

Cole had stopped howling as Pat held him and now sobbed and moaned in his mother's arms. The cemetery was still. The children were all silent, too stunned to even cry, and even the birds—*Buteo jamaicensis, Dendroica petechia, Agelaius phoenicus*—stopped calling to each from the limbs above. The only sound I heard was my own breathing and a humming in my ear as if someone were holding a tuning fork close to my head. Some of the chaperones tried to keep the students away from the corpse, telling them to wait at the bottom of the hill, to not look at Jason, or what was left of him. I didn't do that. I let my kids look. I let them get close, letting them see a real horror story, and hoped I was teaching them something.

Lost Things

Originally anthologized in *Boomtown: Explosive Writing From Ten Years of the Queens University of Charlotte MFA Program*

It was cold the morning of my father's surgery. Wind from Canada swirled across the lake and loosened the last grip of fall. Every brittle leaf that scraped across the pavement reminded me that snow would soon blanket roofs, gutters, and the limbs of skeletal trees. I dreaded winter and already felt weighed down by it all.

I should have welcomed the year coming to a close. It had been a year of loss—first my mother, quickly, quietly in her sleep right after the holidays; then my job at Ford in the spring; and finally Debbie in the summer. It would have been easier if she'd left me for someone younger, or more handsome, or wealthier, but she left me for no one, saying that we'd just grown apart, that she was already alone, and the divorce would just make it legal. Now, in early November, it was just me and Pop, staring down the double barrels of his surgery and the fast-approaching winter.

The doctors had been monitoring the polyp in his colon for a while. The growth was too large to remove by an endoscopic procedure when it was first discovered, and they were hesitant to remove it surgically because of his age, his diabetes, and his heart condition. During the last visit, they told us that the polyp had now grown too large to ignore, that it was probably cancerous, that it should be removed with part of his colon, and that they had to take the risk despite his age. Everyone agreed that even if the surgery were successful, the recovery period would be long and hard. If he did nothing, it would be only a matter of time.

I stood in the driveway waiting, ashing my cigarette while my Ford idled, the heater running, warming the car for him. The Ford's backseat and trunk were loaded with my belongings. I was to move back into the old house, my old room, while he recovered from the surgery, but we both knew I'd have moved back anyway. My house was on the market. Where else could I go but home with him?

Pop came out of the house carrying the duffle bag I'd packed for him. It contained his shaving kit, a change of clothes, his pajamas, the book he was reading, and the black and white photo from his nightstand of my parents honeymooning at Virginia Beach. He locked the back door and walked toward me. His posture had become more stooped in the past year, his body more brittle looking, his gait now a shuffle as he relied more and more on his cane. The winter coat he wore hung off his shoulders, showing the weight he'd lost since last season. The air fogged when he spoke.

"Let's take the Caddy," he said.

"My car's warmed up, Pop."

"That thing's too hard for me to get in and out of. The Cadillac's easier for me."

I pulled my car forward to back the Cadillac around it and opened the door for him. He handed me the duffle bag and sat in the Caddy before swinging in his legs and pulling the door closed. He rested the cane between his legs. I put his bag in the trunk and slid behind the wheel. The car was almost fifteen years old, but my father treated it like he had just driven it off the dealer's lot. My mother hadn't been pleased when he bought the car. She thought it was too big, too expensive, and used too much gas. Why did they need so much car now, at this stage of their lives, she'd wanted to know.

"This is the last car I'm ever going to own. I've always wanted a Cadillac," Pop had answered, and my mother never complained about the car again.

I checked the odometer before pulling out of the driveway. He'd put on twenty-five miles since last week, and I wondered where he'd gone. The doctors had told him not to drive anymore, but I didn't have the stones to take the keys from him.

"How you feeling?" I asked, as I headed toward the corner, the big engine running smooth and quiet even though it was still cold; driving the Cadillac was like steering a couch.

"I'm okay. A little tired. I didn't sleep well."

"You're just nervous about the operation."

He shrugged, his once broad shoulders now lost in the extra material of his winter coat. "Debbie called."

I turned and looked at him. He had shaved that morning and had missed a small patch of white whiskers on his cheek. "She did?"

"She wanted to wish me luck with the operation. Said she'd come visit me."

"That was nice of her."

"She's a nice girl. You need to fix things with her. Talk to her."

"I tried, Pop."

"Try again. Turn left up here."

"Saint Anthony's the other way."

"I want to go by the restaurant first."

"Pop..."

"We got time."

I sighed, glanced at the dashboard clock, shook my head, but turned left at the light and headed deeper into the city, away from Saint Anthony's Hospital.

I parked the Cadillac in front of where the New Genesee restaurant had stood. The front window was boarded up and covered with graffiti; wind-blown garbage—paper cups, hamburger wrappers, dead leaves—had accumulated in the doorway. My father had closed the restaurant and sold the building almost twenty years earlier. Since then the building had been used as a rib joint, a topless bar, and a dirty bookstore before finally becoming vacant. A few summers ago, people had complained of the stench coming from the place, and the police found two bodies inside, both long dead from bad heroin. After Pop read about that in the paper, he stopped talking for two days, keeping whatever pain or anger he felt hidden from Mom and me. Debbie had said I'd inherited that same trait from him. She didn't say it like a compliment.

"That was my bedroom there," he said, leaning across me and pointing with a finger bent by arthritis to a freshly-boarded, second-story window, the dormer around the window charred by a recent fire.

"When your grandfather needed help, he'd grab a broom and tap the ceiling for me to come down. Tap tap tap. He'd have a metal bucket turned over in front of the sink or counter and I'd stand on it and wash dishes or chop onions or whatever was needed. I couldn't have been more than five or six. Sometimes I still wake up thinking I hear that tapping."

I nodded and looked at the clock again; I'd heard all the New Genesee stories a thousand times.

"You see that light pole? The one right there in front of the restaurant?"

"I see it, Pop."

"That's where I fought Jimmy Slattery."

I turned to him. "*You* fought Jimmy Slattery? The lightweight champ?"

He grinned at me. "He wasn't champ when I fought him. He was washed up by then."

"Why'd you fight him?"

"He was drunk and loud and bothering the waitresses, so I took him outside."

"You're kidding me. You took Jimmy Slattery outside? Who won?"

My old man shrugged his thin shoulders and looked embarrassed. "He hit hard for an old drunk." He pointed to a thin scar that bisected his right eyebrow.

"You told me you got that from a door."

"He hit like a door," he said, and we both laughed. "Johnny Manos was a pretty good featherweight, but he was a drunk, too. He fought under the name 'Johnny Mosquito, the Buffalo Torpedo'. Stupidest damn fight name I ever heard. He wore diamond pinky rings and he'd ask me to hold them when he went on a bender so he wouldn't lose them. He said I was the only one in the neighborhood he could trust. I was always nervous when I had them, afraid I'd lose them somehow."

"How long would you hang on to them?"

"Sometimes a week, sometimes two. Once I had them for a month and I was sure he was dead, and I wondered what I should do with them. I didn't know if I should pawn them or what. Then one morning he came in the restaurant looking like hell but alive and sober and asked for them back. He'd always give me a few bucks for keeping them safe. I wonder what happened to those rings. Probably buried with old Johnny years ago."

My father stared at the boarded-up building, lost in his memories until I said, "We should get going, Pop. They want you there early to prep you."

"In a minute. We got time."

"This isn't the best place to be any more."

A bum stumbled around the corner. He shuffled towards us, his hair thick and white, his face pink. A grimy raincoat hung open on his shoulders. He leaned against the boarded-up movie house two doors down from the restaurant and pulled a bottle sleeved in a brown bag from his coat. I hoped Pop wasn't putting those miles on the Cadillac by coming down here alone.

"That was the Palace Theater," Pop said, and I wondered if he saw the drunk at all or if he just remembered the marquee lit by hundreds of colored bulbs. "I met your mother there. She was the ticket girl. Prettiest girl I'd ever seen. There used to be a glass booth out front where she sat. That was a beautiful old place, the Palace. Gold-leaf paint, ruby velvet seats, ceilings painted with stars. Your mother and I saw all the pictures there. Great actors back then, too. Real actors, not those pretty boys you got today. Kirk Douglas, Gregory Peck, Bogart. Robert Mitchum was my favorite."

"I know, Pop, but we got to watch the time."

The drunk stood under the dark and broken marquee and took a long pull on the bottle before putting it back in his coat. He staggered up the sidewalk, his lips moving as if he were talking or singing to himself. His arm shot up and he gestured with his hand and pointed at things that were not there. He stopped in front of the restaurant and stared hard at the boarded-up front window.

I knew what the drunk was going to do before Pop did. I saw him fumble with the rope that held up his greasy pants and turn toward the restaurant. Then Pop saw him.

"Hey." He leaned forward toward the dash, making sure he saw correctly. "Hey!"

"Pop," I said, but he had already flung open the Caddy's door and was struggling to get out.

He was barely standing before he slammed his cane down on the cement with a cracking noise. "Get the hell away from there!"

The cane swung again, this time smashing against the light pole where Jimmy Slattery had scarred him a lifetime ago. The bum jerked toward the noise, spraying urine, and saw Pop coming after him, already choking up on the cane like DiMaggio getting ready to swing for the fences.

I don't remember getting out of the car, just moving fast around the fender to intercept him.

I saw the bum's eyes grow wide. I wasn't sure if it was Pop's yelling or seeing me coming around the front of the Caddy that scared him, but he stuffed himself back in, staining the front of his pants even more, and stumbled up the block trying to retie the rope he used for a belt. I grabbed Pop by the arms; they felt like bones through his sleeves. It was as if my touch drained the life from him; he sagged into his coat and then into me.

"It's okay, Pop. He's gone. You chased him away."

"That son-of-a-bitch," he said, but all the fight was out of his voice. The cold wind watered his eyes but didn't color his face.

"Let's go, Pop. It's all right. We're late already. They're waiting for us."

He let me lead him back to the Cadillac, and he collapsed in the front seat. I closed the heavy door and worried how all the excitement was affecting him physically, hoping the doctors wouldn't have to postpone the surgery because his blood pressure was too high or because his heart rate was too elevated.

I climbed in the driver's side and glanced quickly at him before putting the car in gear. He was sitting far back in the seat, his coat bunching around him, as if swallowing him a body part at a time. His breathing was still coming in fast, shallow clips.

"Do you want to listen to some music, Pop?" I asked, and turned on the radio even though he didn't answer. He had the station tuned to WECK AM 1230, the nostalgia station that played big band and torch music. We listened to *Breakfast with Sinatra*. "One for My Baby" was playing as I steered to the hospital. Pop didn't talk much, only answering my questions with one-word replies or a shake of his head.

I parked in front of St. Anthony's and killed the engine. Pop made no move to get out of the car.

"Don't be upset about that bum. He was just a drunk."

"Robert Mitchum knew what he was doing," he mumbled, looking out the window at the hospital. "He figured it out."

"What are you talking about?"

"They didn't open him up. No prodding and poking by strangers. No in and out of hospitals for the rest of his miserable life like some damn science experiment. He just woke up in the middle of the night and sat in his favorite chair by the window. He lit a cigarette and drank tequila. That's where they found him. The cigarette was still burning in the ashtray. They thought he was sleeping because he looked so peaceful there in his robe."

He turned to me then, his face still drained of color, his eyes still watery. "Dying like you lived is a hell of a thing."

He kept his wet eyes on me. I didn't see fear or anger in them, just a kind of pleading.

"A hell of a thing," he said again, and turned back toward Saint Anthony's.

The hospital loomed above us, its cut limestone looking as cold and gray as the leaden sky that now threatened snow or, worse, freezing rain. A statue of Saint Anthony, the patron saint of lost things, stood by the main entrance, his arms open, his palms turned upward in what was meant as a welcoming gesture but what struck me then as a resigned shrug, a public admission that he couldn't find shit, that once something's lost, it's gone for good.

I glanced down at the gas gauge; the tank was full, and I figured that Cadillac could go about two hundred miles before we'd have to stop and fill it. If I could find the courage, I could see me and Pop heading south, someplace warm, away from winter and heavy coats, maybe someplace on the water like Cape Fear, the title and setting of his favorite Robert Mitchum movie. Just for a second, I pictured Debbie riding with us, the windows open, the warm ocean breeze blowing back her dark hair, but I knew that was asking too much.

We'd rent a cottage or a beach house, maybe do a little fishing off the dock on days when Pop felt up for it. At night I'd push his chair by the window in case he woke and wanted to watch the moon reflect off the shimmering water, have a smoke, and wait.

Ohio Street

Originally published in *The Cleveland Review*

don't recognize the two boys who carry my son. I search their faces for some familiarity, something in the curve of the mouth or the shape of the nose that will remind me that they'd once played soccer with Brandon or had ridden the bus with him to elementary school. Nothing—not the pierced eyebrow of the taller one or the Chinese character tattooed on the shorter one's neck—reminds me of anyone smiling in a team photo or waving goodbye from a bus window. I can't identify a trace of boy in these sullen teenagers who carry my son to the couch without explanation.

"Is he hurt?" my wife asks. Small lines near the corners of her mouth, like cracks, seem more pronounced than I remember.

They drop Brandon on the couch rather than lying him down gently. The smell of liquor seeps through my son's pores and fills the living room with each exhaled breath. The two boys wordlessly pass me, probably wishing they'd left Brandon on the front porch instead of carrying him inside; their clothes smell of marijuana as they slide by, turning their shoulders to avoid touching me.

"He's okay," I answer. "Just drunk. Passed out."

The shorter boy, the one with the tattoo, snickers.

"What's your name?" I ask, my voice loud and sharp. "Are you the Sutter boy? Jim's son?"

They hurry out the door, leaving me standing in the middle of the living room clenching and unclenching my fists.

Katherine sits on the edge of the couch and touches Brandon's hair, his face, his shoulders, checking for damage. "Are you sure he's not hurt?"

"He'll be fine. I'll sit with him. Get some sleep."

Katherine frowns, deepening those lines that have appeared so suddenly and uninvited, like the gray hair silvering my temples.

When did we get old?

When did Brandon?

"Wake me if you need me, all right?" She rises and heads to the stairs, rubbing my shoulder as she passes. There's sadness in her touch, an acknowledgment that we're moving together into a new phase of parenting, a phase we're not quite prepared for.

From our driveway, an engine roars to life. I don't know the make—Ford, Chevy, Plymouth—but I know the type without looking: a teenager's first set of wheels, the kind that barely passes inspection, the kind that my buddy Sean and I had when we were Brandon's age. I'm not surprised to hear the tires squeal or the horn held in a continual blare as the boys peal down the street, probably with the headlights doused.

I'd have done the same thing.

The house is quiet after Katherine goes upstairs and the engine fades. I turn to Brandon. His shoes, unlaced army boots, are caked with mud, and I wonder where he's been, imagining him vomiting in bushes or passed out on some lawn after a night of birthday drinking with friends I do not know. The boots slip off easily, and I take them to the front hall, locking the door and turning off the porch light before returning to the living room.

Then I do something that would've horrified me if my father had done it to me when I was sixteen; I go through my son's pockets. I start with his gray hoodie, looking for. . .what? A bowl? A nickel bag? Condoms? His jacket yields nothing but a few crumpled dollars, a package of mints, and a one-ounce bottle of Visine.

They haven't changed the label in thirty years.

Like a cop, I pat the front of his jeans, expecting to feel the outline of a lighter or a plastic pill bottle through the faded denim. All I feel is his cell phone and pull it out and place it on the coffee table. I roll Brandon onto his side and shove my hand in his back pocket and tug his wallet out. I open it and find seven more crumpled dollars and a slip of paper with Linda written in a girl's swirling hand above a phone number, the "i" in her name dotted with a heart. I flip through the plastic credit card slots, searching for rolling papers or a joint. I find nothing, just his high school ID, his library card, and the learner's permit that he'd gotten earlier this afternoon, the afternoon of his birthday. I had offered to drive him, but he said a buddy would take him. I hope Linda, who signs her name with floating hearts, gave him a ride to the DMV.

I toss the wallet on the coffee table next to his phone and sit in a chair facing the couch, leaving Brandon unconscious on his side, realizing I'm different from my father. I know what to look for. If either of my parents had found my bottle of Visine when I was in high school, I would have mumbled something about allergies or hay fever and they would have believed me. What else could possibly bloodshot a teenager's eyes?

The chair squeaks as I shift my weight. Tomorrow, when Brandon is sober, I'll need to talk to him. What will I say? What *can* I say? Who the hell am I to lecture anyone?

I try not to think of Sean, but that's impossible. I'd known all the old memories would flare as soon as I'd heard that engine rumble to life in my driveway. I can picture us impossibly young, our bodies tan and hard, bent under the hood of that Dodge, working on it every chance we got.

"I love this car," Sean always said. "A 440 under the hood, eight cylinders, pure Detroit muscle."

"She's still not running right," I'd answer, adjusting the carb, or dicking with the fuel pump, or playing with the belts, or whatever I was trying to fix while Sean went on about our car.

Technically, Sean owned the Charger; the title was in his name, but it was *our* car. We bought it off of Chuck Mancuso the summer Sean and I turned seventeen and kept it up on blocks in Sean's driveway while we worked on it. We used parts we found at my uncle's junkyard—a radiator, a passenger-side door, front seats—and tools Sean borrowed from his father's collision shop. Sean's dad would order the parts we couldn't find, so we only paid wholesale, or Sean would just take them from the storeroom when his dad wasn't around. We worked on the car most of the summer, pouring every dime we had into it, busting our knuckles when a wrench slipped, trying hard to get the grease off our hands at night but never getting it all, so our palms were constantly black-lined.

The only book we cracked open that summer was *Chilton's Auto Repair*.

It took us until mid-August before the Charger could even pass inspection. By then, the days had already grown shorter.

Sean didn't want to take it out that night; that was my idea. He wanted to paint it first and not let anyone see it until we pulled into the school's parking lot on the first day with the engine revving.

"They'll all come up to us," he'd said. "They'll want to touch it, run their hands along the fenders and finger the chrome. They'll want to hear the engine and ask to drive it, but we won't let them."

I couldn't blame him for wanting to paint it first. The Charger's original color was bright blue, but our passenger side door was white and the hood tan, both parts cannibalized from wrecked Chargers at the junkyard. The tire wells were black-primed where we'd cut out the rust and fitted new metal. It needed to be painted, but I couldn't wait.

I was seventeen and the summer night was warm with possibilities. So I talked Sean into it, and we cruised around town, drinking from sweating beer bottles and doing one-hitters at stoplights. I was driving and felt as powerful as the horsepower under the hood.

I don't remember whose idea it was to go to Ohio Street.

We'd talked about it enough during all those days we worked on the Charger. "We'll take on all comers…"

"…shut them down one after the other…"

"…then spray paint our initials under the bridge."

In the 70's, Ohio Street was a lonely stretch of road flanked by abandoned warehouses. When manufacturing headed south, there was nothing left to warehouse, so the red brick buildings were boarded up and the gates padlocked. It was one of those forgotten roads perfect for street racing. Nobody went down there. There was no reason to, except to race.

We'd heard all the stories from the older guys who hung out at the junkyard scavenging parts for their own cars, how they ran for pinks or money, and how every summer someone would spin out or flip over when he hit the bend right after the overpass. I wasn't worried about wrecking or winning any money. I just wanted to see how fast the Charger could go.

"Are we early?" Sean asked, as we turned onto Ohio Street.

"Maybe we're late."

"It's not even dark yet. Maybe they don't race every night."

I pulled on my beer and gunned the engine, the only noise down there.

"So what do you want to do?"

"Let's just wait and see if anyone shows," I said.

We sat on that forgotten road with the engine idling and drank warm beer and smoked dope as the skies darkened and those haunted looking warehouses receded into shadows. We listened to the radio, argued about bands, talked about girls, and waited for someone to show. Nobody did, and I begin to wonder if Ohio Street racing was just junkyard talk.

"Fuck it," I said, after a while. "Let's race anyway."

"Against who?"

"Us."

I pressed the accelerator until the RPM needle redlined and then popped the clutch. The tires squealed and smoked and the Charger hurtled forward.

"Christ," Sean said, spilling his beer.

I ran through the gears, watching the speedometer climb, wanting to see where we'd top out.

Thirty.

Forty.

The needle mesmerized me.

Sixty.

The power vibrated in my crotch. Sean rebel yelled out the window, the wind blowing back the sound and his hair.

Seventy-five.

We rocketed under the overpass covered in graffiti.

Eighty.

We rounded the bend.

And there he was.

Frozen.

His rusting shopping cart on the shoulder filled with empty bottles.

Still holding the beer can he'd retrieved from the middle of Ohio Street.

Wearing a green army jacket in the middle of August.

I stood on the brake pedal, the squealing tires mixing with our screams as I fought the wheel. The air filled with the smell of burning brake pads and spilled beer. I saw the curly hair that hung to his shoulders, his scruffy beard, his accepting expression.

The Charger smashed into him at eighty-five miles an hour with a haunting, soul-leaving sound of an exploding headlight, twisting metal, and shattering bones.

I was six blocks away before I pulled over.

"Jesus. Jesus. Jesus," Sean kept repeating. Tears ran down his face. "Jesus."

"I couldn't stop. I was going too fast. He was just there."

"Jesus."

"What are we going to do?"

"I don't know. Jesus."

A siren wailed and Sean and I looked at each other, his eyes big and wet like they were made of pure pupil. The siren grew louder as it neared us. It was moving fast.

"Christ."

We saw the fire truck turn onto Ohio Street and race away from us, the siren's wail fading as the distance between us grew.

I opened the door and leaned out, retching until there was nothing left.

"We got to get out of here," Sean said.

Two days passed before a highway crew found the body. A small article appeared in the paper about the unknown man found alongside Ohio Street. The police asked for people to come forward if they had any information on the hit-and-run or the identity of the victim.

Nobody thought it strange that we replaced the Charger's bumper, grill, and headlight; we'd spent all summer swapping out parts from the junkyard. Sean's old man said we should have painted it bright blue like the factory original, but we told him black was much cooler, that the girls would love it. He shook his head and muttered, *Kids*.

My stomach lurched each time our phone rang or someone knocked on the door.

A week later there was a second article. The police had identified him from VA records: Robert J. Simmons. Twenty-nine years old. Address and next-of-kin unknown. He had survived two tours in Viet Nam only to be killed on Ohio Street.

There were no more articles after that.

Before school started, Sean and I sold the Charger to his cousin from Pennsylvania who had come up for Labor Day. We split the money.

The nightmares started right after. Sometimes the collision would play out as it happened, but other times the Charger would be caught in an endless skid, the tires screeching, the brakes trying to grip, and Robert Simmons would just stand there, staring at me through the windshield, holding that beer can, waiting for the impact that never comes. Even now I'll sometimes wake up screaming and Katherine will hold me, wipe my face with soft palms, and beg me to tell what's in my dreams.

I always answer that I don't remember.

I didn't see much of Sean after we sold the car. Everyone thought we'd drifted apart because we didn't have the Charger anymore, but we drifted apart because the Charger was always between us. After we sold it, we never spoke about that night again, as if our silence could bury what had happened.

Brandon rolls over on his back and moans in his drunken sleep, pulling me away from that damn Charger. I move to him and sit on the edge of the couch. He groans again, this boy, my boy, the child I've kept safe and protected for sixteen years, the one who thinks I give money to the homeless because I'm a good man. How will he think of me tomorrow if I tell him about Ohio Street, if I warn him about what can happen when he's out trying to see how fast he can go?

I brush the hair from his forehead and let my fingers trail down his cheek, dreading the moment when he opens his eyes.

The Corner of
Walnut and Vine

Originally published in *Blackheart Magazine*

I could smell the shampoo from my wife's hair as she leaned into me to look out the driver's side window.

"Honey, look," she said, pointing at an open house sign. "It's perfect. Pull over."

She shifted away and opened the door.

"Jesus. Wait a second."

I steered the car towards the curb and hoped this wasn't a new version of an old game she liked to play. Nikki liked to wander the mall, trying on leather coats we couldn't afford, marveling at flat screen TVs and shaking her head at the prices of cribs, bassinets, and baby clothes.

She was already out of the car and heading toward the house before I'd killed the engine. The autumn wind carried the smell of burning leaves and fireplaces as I climbed out of the Buick and walked to where she stood. She was shaking. I slipped my arm around her waist and pulled her to me.

"Look at it," she said. "Just look at it."

The house was a two-story English Cape, or so Nikki told me, that stood on the corner of Walnut and Vine, directly across from McCarthy Park. A waist-high hedge encircled the front lawn and was only broken at the walk by a white arbor; rose bushes intertwined through the lattice. The flowers were mostly gone, leaving behind stems and thorns.

"Can we go in?" she asked, but she had already slipped free.

I followed her as far as the arbor. She called over her shoulder that the stucco looked freshly painted.

"We should go, Nikki," I said, but it was too late.

The door opened, and a middle-aged woman dressed in gray stood in the doorway. She introduced herself as Ellen Daly, the listing agent, her gaze flitting past us, taking in my car with a quick glance.

"I'm Nikki and this is my husband, Tim," Nikki said.

They both looked at me from the steps, their smiles pulling me through that damn arbor and up the walk. Ellen had a strong grip for a woman, as if all the years of standing in doorways and shaking hands of people who didn't want to be there had strengthened her fingers.

"I didn't think anyone would stop by today," she said, moving aside so we could enter the house. "I think everyone's home watching football."

I forced a smile and squeezed past as Nikki sucked in her breath. The hallway floor was slate and the walls wood-lined.

Nikki ran her hand lightly over the wainscoting, her fingers barely brushing the surface. "Is this paneling or tongue and groove?"

"Tongue and groove," the realtor answered. "It's an addition, but the owners didn't scrimp on anything, as you can see."

Tongue and groove? How did my wife know to ask such a question?

We entered the living room, and Nikki slipped her right hand into my left; her other hand squeezed my upper arm, the happy couple out house-hunting on a Sunday afternoon.

Christ.

"That's a working fireplace. The chimney was just recently repointed," Ellen said.

"It's gorgeous," Nikki answered, breaking away from me again and heading toward the mantle. She reached out to touch the wood, as if she wouldn't believe anything in the house were real unless she felt it.

"What's the square footage?" she asked over her shoulder.

"Seventeen-hundred square feet of livable space. It's small, but I think it's just darling for a young couple starting out."

Both Nikki and Ellen turned to me and waited for me to ask a question.

"How old is it?" was the best I could do.

"About sixty years but very well maintained. I don't think you'll find a place with a better location. Did you have a chance to walk through the park? It'll be right outside your front door."

"It's beautiful," Nikki said.

Ellen nodded. "Especially this time of year when the leaves are changing. Of course it's pretty in the winter, too, when the evergreens are covered in snow. It's like a Christmas card. There's skating on the duck pond when it's cold enough."

Nikki smiled at me before wandering into the dining room. "Are the current owners a young couple, too?" she asked.

Photocopies listing recent repairs were stacked on the table. Nikki took one. I raised my wrist and showed Nikki my watch, but she ignored me.

"No. Mrs. Menza is a widow, in her seventies. She just bought a small one-story home near her daughter."

It didn't surprise me that the owner was older. The furniture was dark and out of style. Framed needlepoints hung on the wall, and the mantle was covered with photographs of smiling children. The house had that grandmother smell to it, a mix of Mentholatum, potpourri, and windows that had been shut for too long.

"When does she close on the other house?" my wife asked, folding her arms across her chest as she stood in front of the dining room table.

"I believe she closes in a few weeks."

"So she's anxious to sell," Nikki said.

"I think she'd like to have this place sold by then, yes," Ellen answered, and we both followed my wife into the kitchen.

"Is there a basement?" Nikki asked, as she took in the kitchen and small breakfast nook with a sweeping glance.

"Yes, but it's unfinished. Of course there are washer and dryer hookups and stationary tubs down there." Ellen opened a door and flipped on the basement light.

Nikki turned to me. "Honey, why don't you check the cellar while Ellen shows me the kitchen."

I glared at her and headed downstairs.

"Feel the walls for dampness and make sure the wiring's up to code," Nikki called after me.

I stood in the middle of the basement and listened to the drifting murmur of my wife's voice and Ellen's laughter.

Check the wiring to make sure it's up to code?

Jesus.

I lit a cigarette, ashing it quickly to the filter. The longer we stayed in the house, the angrier I became. Nikki truly wanted to know about the wiring and the age of the hot water tank, but the only thing I wanted to know was what the hell she was thinking. Maybe in a few years we could manage a down payment, but not now, not with the bills we had. Each step I took in the basement was a step I couldn't afford. The hot water tank, the furnace, even the goddamn stationary tubs were all out of reach.

And Nikki knew it.

I didn't know how long I should stay in the basement or even what to look for, so I smoked another cigarette, taking my time with this one, before climbing the stairs.

I wandered around the first floor looking for them and peeked into a small book-lined den. I heard their voices on the second level and went up and found them in the smallest of the three bedrooms.

"…perfect for a nursery," I heard Ellen say as I entered the room.

"There you are," Nikki said, and kissed my cheek. "I thought you got lost. How was the basement?"

"The walls were dry," I reported.

"The furnace was replaced about eighteen months ago," Ellen said. "The combined heating and electric bill is around $300 a month, but you have to remember that Mrs. Menza is older and had the thermostat set slightly higher. Of course, she was home all day. That makes a difference."

Nikki nodded in agreement. "A big difference."

I trailed behind as I was shown the other two bedrooms with "plenty of closet space, plenty", the full bath, a cedar closet, and other ground they had already covered. This time it was Nikki, not Ellen, who pointed out each room or feature to me, her words rushing together, defying punctuation.

"Now that only leaves the backyard," Ellen said to us after we took turns sticking our heads through the ceiling to inspect the crawlspace and the thickness of the goddamn insulation. She smiled and raised an eyebrow as if she were about to reveal national secrets. We followed her downstairs and through the kitchen. While Ellen fiddled with the back door, Nikki explained that Mrs. Menza planned on leaving all the appliances, including the refrigerator. She stood beside me, shifting her weight from one foot to the other.

"Mrs. Menza," Ellen said, finally opening the door, "is quite the accomplished gardener."

We stepped into the backyard. The lawn, although small, was thick and green, but the flowerbeds were a smear of yellows, pinks, and purples. A sundial, something I hadn't seen in years, stood in the middle of the grass, and a birdbath was tucked in the corner near the back wall.

"The purple ones are asters," Ellen said, pointing towards the fence. "That's sedum right next to them. Goldenrod forms a nice border, don't you think? And you recognize the mums, I bet. Of course you're only getting half the effect. Fall flowers are nice, but wait until spring when everything blooms."

"My God," were the only words Nikki could say.

We followed Ellen around the side of the house, where she pointed out more perennials and annuals and Mrs. Menza's vegetable garden; she made sure I noticed the new gutters and downspouts. Nikki trailed us, quieter now, as reality rushed back at her. When we reached the sidewalk, Ellen asked if we had more questions or if we wanted to go back inside for another look. I said no, and she handed me her business card and a sheet of financial information about the asking price, down payments, and fixed-rate mortgages.

"And remember," Ellen said, looking me in the eye. "Mrs. Menza is asking less than the appraised value, so your taxes will likely go down."

I nodded, as if turning that bit of financial information around in my head and mentally chewing it over, as if it mattered.

Ellen took turns shaking our hands before we climbed into the Buick. Nikki watched Ellen walk back to the house to wait for another couple.

"Well," I said, turning the ignition. The car rumbled to life; the patch on the muffler had worked free.

"Well," Nikki repeated in a voice so small and sad I had to turn to her. She smiled then, the same smile I had seen my mother give my father a thousand times while I was growing up. There were never any fights between them, no major ones anyway. There was just that smile containing all the quietly accepted disappointments that he and life had given her. I finally understood why sometimes, when my father thought he was alone and drifted deep in his own thoughts, he'd shake his head, and his shoulders would sag, as if burdened by all those things he couldn't deliver.

"Well," I said again, unable to think of anything to say or do except jerk the car in gear, smile my father's smile, and head toward home.

Culling

Originally published in *Rosebud*

I began running because I had nothing better to do. I never mapped my route or planned the distance beforehand; I took whatever turn or path struck me and ran until I grew tired. Running was the only time I wouldn't think about how I couldn't afford school anymore, or find full-time work, or how my closest friends were all leaving town—Brent for the air force, Matthew to work for his brother out west, Gregg down to Virginia to live with some girl. They couldn't find work, either. Ford and American Axle had all had multiple layoffs that year. Rumors were swirling that Bethlehem Steel was shutting down for good. My Uncle Mike had been laid off from GM for so long his benefits were running out. So I'd run in the mornings and dry cars at Delta Sonic in the afternoons. The girls I worked with would bend to wipe fenders in their tight blue pants and received the most tips. The more ambitious ones wore shorts despite the cool spring temperatures.

One morning I found myself running through Delaware Park and around the boarded-up casino, heading towards the man-made lake adjacent to the expressway. I never made it that far. The path to Hoyt Lake was so clogged with geese and splattered excrement that I had to stop. I stood breathing hard, my hands on my hips, my calf starting to cramp, and took in the scene. Down drifted in the air like gray snowflakes; a slick film floated on the water's surface. The honking was constant.

"It's awful, isn't it, Ricky?" a familiar voice asked. Sal sat on a park bench holding a copy of the *Courier Express*, the morning paper that would go out of business a year later.

I'd known Sal since I was a kid. He was a fixture at Quinn's, my Uncle Mike's favorite bar. His face was deeply creased as if someone had chiseled away at him, leaving deep furrows across his forehead and cascading down his cheeks. Wispy white hair poked under his Local 774 ball cap, the same hat my uncle sometimes wore.

"Where did they come from, Sal?" I asked, my words uneven as I tried to catch my breath.

"They're heading north. The paper says the grass running to the water's edge naturally attracts them. The flocks may be resting before they go on to Canada. Some might even fly as far as Alaska."

"Jesus, there's so many."

"More come every day."

"Can't the City do something? Or the Parks Department?"

Sal shook his head. "They brought a dog out. A border collie. He ran around and barked a lot. Didn't do much good. The geese barked back. There's talk of addling their eggs now."

"What does that mean?"

"Damned if I know, but they better do something quick. They're taking over the goddamn place."

I watched the biggest and loudest goose strut and chase the others in a harsh mix of honking and flapping before I stretched a little and limped home.

The next day I went to visit Uncle Mike. The houses on his street looked like ungaraged cars, faded and rusting around the edges. Front porches buckled and needed replacing; paint bubbled and peeled around the trim. Yellowed newspapers, flattened Styrofoam cups, and tossed beer cans revealed by melted snow clustered under bushes and at the base of budding trees. Fresh tire tracks rutted across my uncle's front lawn and continued through the hedge and across his neighbor's yard. It had rained earlier that morning, and the tracks were now muddy gashes. He was sitting on the front steps, his M1 carbine from the War (he never called it World War II) broken down around him.

"They did a number on your lawn, Uncle Mike," I said, getting out of my mother's Impala and walking toward him.

He took a swig of Utica Club before saying, "The neighborhood's gone to hell, Ricky Boy." He set the beer next to the other empty bottles.

"It was just kids," I said, looking at the tire tracks.

Uncle Mike shrugged and lit a cigarette. He offered me the pack, but I shook my head; I'd given them up when I started running.

"Where you been?" he asked. "You working?"

"Just at Delta Sonic. Part time."

"Better than nothing," he said, squinting through cigarette smoke and rubbing his side where there'd once been bone. During the War, his jeep had struck a land mine. He'd been thrown clear but impaled on a picket fence. When I was a kid, he'd take me to Crystal Beach or swimming at the North Buffalo Y and would catch me staring at that ugly scar. He'd tell me to make a fist and press it in for luck. My hand would sink in the soft flesh where the ribs had been removed.

"I didn't know you still had that," I said, nodding to the rifle. "Will it shoot?"

Uncle Mike ran a rod down the barrel, the wet patch affixed to the end breaking up the old powder and lead residue. "Sure it will. Once I clean it."

"Who you gonna shoot? The kid who ruined your lawn?"

He shook his head. "I'm going to shoot those damn geese by the lake. A little girl got bit on the thigh yesterday. Four years old. I saw it on the news."

I waited for him to smile or wink or somehow let me know he was joking. He just removed the dirty wet patch and replaced it with a dry one.

"You can't shoot birds in a public park, Uncle Mike. You'll get arrested," I said, realizing he was serious. "And even if you could, you can't shoot geese with that thing. You'll blow them in half."

"Damn right I will." He ran the rod down the barrel again, the new patch soaking up the excess solvent and remaining dirt.

"There'll be people around. Someone's gonna get hurt."

"Only the geese are going to get hurt, Ricky Boy. I was a good shot in the War."

"That was almost forty years ago."

"Some things don't change." He began to assemble the carbine.

"Jesus, how many are you going to kill?"

"As many as I can before the rest fly off. Then they'll never come back. They'll know the lake isn't safe anymore."

I studied my uncle as he put the old rifle back together. His face was the color of cigarette ash. My mother worried he hadn't been eating; he'd been turning down her dinner invitations. Nicotine had stained his fingertips yellow and discolored his teeth. I wondered if he'd been surviving on unfiltered Camels and Utica Club. He wheezed as he refitted the butt plate.

"What do you say we head to Quinn's and shoot some pool?" I asked, afraid he'd head to the park and start blasting as soon as the rifle was assembled. "We could get something to eat. A fish fry or something."

"Sure," he said, his stained fingers moving quickly. I was certain he could still assemble the rifle in the dark if he had to.

When he finished, he grabbed the porch railing and pulled himself to his feet. He wavered, and I reached out to steady him.

"Sonofabitch," he said, swatting my hand away. He headed to the hedge gripping the M1, looking like he wanted to shoot more than birds.

I hadn't noticed the extent of the damage before. The grass, with care, could be revived, but the hedge was another matter. The car had barreled through the bushes separating the neighbor's property from his; loose leaves were scattered, and branches were snapped and strewn. Some of the bushes were crushed and uprooted, exposing roots flattened and torn by grinding rear tires.

"I planted these shrubs when I first moved here," Uncle Mike said, staring at the ruined hedge. "Watered the goddamn things and kept them trimmed. Covered them with Christmas lights when you were a kid. Look at them now."

"Maybe we can save them."

"Not even Christ could save these, Ricky Boy. He couldn't save any of this."

Quinn's Pitcher's Mound was one of the bars my uncle took me to when I was a kid. He'd pick me up on Saturdays in his green Chevy Caprice and we'd go there or one of the other bars on Military Road, like Cassatta's or the Military Grill, to get what he called "walking around money". He'd take on all comers at the pool table. I'd sit on a stool, skinny legs dangling, drinking glass after glass of Loganberry Juice, a sickly sweet drink bottled not too far from my house. Uncle Mike would call out his shots to me—"Corner pocket, Ricky Boy", "Three in the side", "Combo off the six"—until he'd drop the eight and yell, "Rack 'em, Ricky Boy," his voice booming above the jukebox and the conversations around us. I'd slide off the stool and rack the balls in a tight triangle like he'd taught me, as he drained another sweating bottle of Utica Club. The dollars he won would disappear into his pocket; the coins would slip into mine. When daylight faded, we'd climb back in the Caprice and weave our way home.

Quinn's was almost empty when we arrived. The layoffs were hurting the Military Road bars as much as they were hurting families. Sal was sitting at his usual spot on the last stool and nodded at us when we walked through the door. Uncle Mike went over, slapped his back, and began talking to the old man while I ordered a couple drafts. Two guys about my age were shooting pool. They wore sweaters over polo shirts with turned up collars, and I wondered what the hell they were doing on Military Road. They belonged at one of the bars near the college, not at a workingman's tavern that served fried bologna sandwiches and displayed jars of pickled eggs on the counter. They were big fuckers, too, with broad shoulders and thick necks, muscles grown from lifting weights, not from manual labor. The shorter one racked the balls, and the redhead's break sounded like a gunshot. Uncle Mike turned when he heard it and watched the balls split and spread across the green felt.

"Nice break, kid," Uncle Mike said.

The redhead didn't answer; instead, he bent to take his next shot.

After Uncle Mike finished talking to Sal and slid onto the stool next to me, he turned slightly so he could watch the pool table.

"That redhead shoots a good stick," he said.

"He's a jerk."

"You know him?"

I shrugged. "I know guys like him. From college. They're pricks."

Uncle Mike nodded and sipped his beer. "You should go back to school, Ricky Boy. Finish up. Become a prick." He smiled, showing his nicotine teeth.

"I need money for that."

"I'd help you if I could," he said, over the sound of ricocheting balls.

"I know."

"There's got to be jobs somewhere."

We both watched the redhead sink a nice two-ball combo, the fifteen dropping quietly in the pocket, before I said, "I'm thinking of heading south, Uncle Mike."

His face caved and looked as old as Sal's, like I had just taken a chisel to him, too. "South?"

I nodded. "The Carolinas maybe. That's where all the jobs are going."

He reached in his jacket for his Camels. His hand shook when he lit the match. "You tell your mother yet?"

"Not yet."

Twin smoke streams shot through his nostrils. "So you're leaving."

"I'm just thinking about it."

He nodded, took a long drink from his beer, almost empting the mug. The redhead sank three balls in a row before leaving the five ball hanging on the edge of the pocket. "I don't blame you, Rick. There's nothing left here. It's all gone to shit."

The shorter one scratched on his first shot, and the redhead laughed.

Uncle Mike and I had a couple more beers and didn't say much after that. I could tell he was thinking about what life would be like without me around, but at least it was better than thinking about shooting geese and going to jail. The guilt I felt about leaving my mother and uncle alone had been weighing me down; speaking my intentions increased the weight, but I didn't know what else to do. Options, like jobs, were scarce.

We watched the two college kids shoot pool until Uncle Mike slapped the bar with his palms and whispered that it was time to teach the prick a lesson. He walked over to the table, his gait wobbly, and asked the redhead if he wanted to shoot a game for a little money.

"I don't want to take your social security check, Mike," he said, reading my uncle's name stitched over the heart of his UAW jacket.

The way the prick pronounced my uncle's name, drawing out the "M" and making a hard "k" sound in the back of his throat, made me want to grab a cue and bash in his red head. Uncle Mike had heard it, too. His body stiffened. Maybe if this had been back in the Loganberry days, he'd have dropped the kid on the spot. Instead, he reached in his pocket and slapped a twenty on the table. I'd never seen him bet that much on a single game before.

The redhead whistled, and the shorter one handed his cue to Uncle Mike. "You can break," the prick said, opening his wallet for a twenty.

"We'll shoot for it," my uncle said, but the redhead just waved him off as his friend racked the balls.

Uncle Mike sank one ball on the break and then two more before missing a bank shot I'd seen him make a thousand times.

"Not bad, Mike," the college kid said, the "k" hard again. He chalked his cue, then began running the table, calling his pocket every time, the balls dropping in one after the other.

Uncle Mike's lips were pressed into a bloodless line as he watched the redhead line up each shot, the cue ball rolling to a stop in perfect position for the next one, until he slammed the eight in the corner harder than needed.

The redhead grinned at my uncle. "Double or nothin'?"

My uncle nodded once and the shorter kid racked the balls again. Uncle Mike never got a chance to shoot in the second game. The redhead was a machine, never missing. He moved around the table quickly, chalking his cue between shots, never once taking his eyes off the felt until the eight ball dropped and the only balls left on the green were my uncle's.

"Again?" the prick asked, looking up and arching one almost-white eyebrow.

Uncle Mike nodded.

"Double or nothing, right?"

"Uncle Mike," I called, trying to save him. "Let's go eat. I'm starving."

"Double or nothing," my uncle said.

"Let's see the money first, Mike."

Uncle Mike had to dig in all his pockets and borrow some from Sal before he came up with eighty crumpled dollars.

"Good man," the prick said.

The redhead's break was even louder this time, the balls spreading across the table as if they were trying to escape. None fell, but a few stopped just short of the pocket's lip. My uncle sank those first, and I heard the redhead mutter *Cherry picking old man* under his breath. His friend laughed. Mike sliced his next shot too thin and scratched. I knew he wouldn't get another shot. The redhead ran the table again; the sound of balls striking was like nails being driven into bone. The game ended quickly.

The short one scooped up their winnings and the pair was smart enough to head to the door. The redhead turned and called over his shoulder, "Thanks for the money, Big Mike," the "k" hanging in the air, and they were gone.

Uncle Mike laid his cue down on the table and moved back to his stool like he was wading through mud, his eyes meeting no one's. He slid next to me and then started ordering bourbon.

Hours later I drove him home, the idea of food waved away each time I mentioned it. He'd mutter unintelligibly, his head lolling as I negotiated turns, his breathing labored and smelling of whiskey. When I pulled into his driveway, I finally made out what he was mumbling— Geese. Goddamn geese.

I hadn't drunk nearly as much as my uncle had, but I struggled running the next morning. My muscles never loosened, and I never fell into an easy stride. Breathing came in gasps, as if there weren't enough oxygen in the world for me. I cut my run short but still headed towards Hoyt Lake, fearing I'd hear rifle fire as I neared or, worse, find a lake full of slaughtered geese, their blood staining the water and my uncle being taken away in handcuffs. That fist finally loosened when I rounded the casino and heard the birds' loud and insistent honking from a half block away.

Sal sat on the park bench, his paper folded on his lap. He stood when he saw me and hurried toward the jogging path. I slowed to a walk and stopped in front of him, my hands on my knees, my lungs burning.

"Rick," he said. "I didn't know how to get hold of you."

I could only cough in response, my breathing and heart rate too high. The geese were shifting around us like the flock was one living creature and not made up of individual birds. The smell of feathers and excrement was so strong I could taste it.

"Your uncle came by my house this morning. The sun wasn't even up yet. Looked like hell, too. Eyes all red and his hair messed up. I think he was still drunk. Wanted to know if I had any .30 caliber ammo he could borrow for that old M1 of his."

I straightened and felt that invisible fist grip me again. "Did you have any?"

"Yeah, a bunch, but he only wanted one round."

My breathing still came in gasps. "Just one?"

Old Sal nodded, his eyes watery red. "I couldn't stop him, Rick. I tried. I swear to God I tried."

I remember sprinting, the sudden movement scaring the geese so they waddled away from me. My legs protested, but I ignored them and headed towards my uncle's house, certain I couldn't keep that pace for long. At any moment I expected my body to fail and shut down, forcing me to stop or collapse on the sidewalk. Instead I slipped into a newly discovered gear, where oxygen flowed and each separate movement of my body—my pounding heart, my contracting and expanding lungs, my working muscles—blended in harmony. I was no longer running aimlessly; I was running toward something. A kind of deafness took hold of me then, blocking out revved engines and squealed brakes and children's laughter as I ran by. I only heard a pulsing in my ears, steady and strong, each beat of pumped blood whispering *faster, faster, faster,* like I couldn't get there soon enough.

Slip Kid

Originally published in *Hunger Mountain*

Slip kid, slip kid, second generation
Only halfway up the tree
—Pete Townshend

My bedroom walls are covered with posters of my heroes: Pete Townshend windmilling his guitar; Roger Daltrey clutching a microphone to his mouth; Keith Moon flailing on his drum kit, his arms a blur. I'm listening to their latest album, the volume kept low because my mother is already asleep across the hall. My head is fuzzy from too much beer and too much weed. I think I hear my old man running up the stairs. Then I hear him calling my mother's name, and I know some serious shit must be hitting the fan. The old man never runs.

Then I'm running, too, to see what's going on, hoping I don't smell like dope. The old man is already filling the stairway when I get to the hall. The Greeks call him *Tavros*—Bull—because his shoulders and arms are so heavily muscled from years of heaving tool cases down at the warehouse. He stands on the top of the step, his collar loosened, his face stroke red.

Mother comes out of their bedroom, her hair mussed from the pillows. Without makeup, she looks haggard, her face drawn and colorless.

"Paul?" she asks.

The old man's thick chest heaves with each breath.

"Paul?" she asks again, louder.

He raises both arms and turns his calloused palms upward before letting them fall. "They shot Father George," he says, and the first thing I think is, *Billy, what the fuck did you do?*

Mother covers her mouth, her eyes blackening to puddles. Before the old man can tell us more, a piercing scream from *Yiayia*, my grandmother, cuts through the house, pushing every other sound right out the damn walls.

We find her lying in bed propped by two pillows, the room dark except for the flickering black-and-white television on her dresser. An arthritic hand points toward the TV. Mother rushes to her and sits with one arm around her shoulders, pulling her close. I stand shaking beside the old man, feeling smaller than I usually do next to his bulk, and stare at the screen. I recognize the gray cut-limestone of our church. The camera pans the parking lot, and then focuses on a sign, *Reserved For Pastor*; Father George's Toyota is parked in front of it. The camera cuts to footage of a body on a gurney being rushed toward an ambulance with its back doors swung wide. One paramedic trots alongside, holding a bag of plasma above the body. The gurney stops and another paramedic pounds on Father George's chest.

"Mother of God," the old man whispers in Greek. He places a hand on my shoulder and squeezes, as if grasping for something solid to hold onto. I swear to Christ the only thing keeping me standing is his grip.

Yiayia makes the sign of the cross in Orthodox fashion, right to left. Her lips move in silent prayer as she crosses herself three times. Her whole body is shaking like she has palsy or something, and now I'm scared the news is too much for her.

Goddamn you, Billy.

Mother's tears catch the TV's flickering light. "We have to call somebody. Somebody must know something."

"Yes." Father straightens. "Yes."

This new mission of discovering the details of the shooting revitalizes him. The old man strides from the room as if he plans to call Billy himself. I lean against the wall, my head buzzing worse than before, wishing I could be absorbed into the floral wallpaper that's hung in this room for as long as I can remember. I choke down the bile.

Yiayia pulls away from Mother and shoves her blankets aside. Her yellow-white hair, normally rolled tight in a bun, hangs loose to her shoulders. She shuffles to her altar, a small table covered with a white cloth; icons of Jesus the Teacher and Saint Peter hang above it. Resting on the table are her worn Bible, a small vial of Holy Water, a blood-red egg wrapped in white mesh from the previous Easter, and her *Candelie*. She lights the candle and starts praying in Greek, but I'm thinking it's too late for that.

Mother and I leave her mumbling in front of the icons and head downstairs, where the phonebook lies open on the kitchen table. The old man hates the phone and holds the receiver in his thick hand away from his face. Clipped bursts of Greek shoot from his mouth like rounds from an Uzi. I can only make out a few words. I sit at the table and listen ignorantly while he rattles into the phone. His muscles tense and bunch beneath his clothes as if he's about to rip the damn phone right off the kitchen wall.

Mother sits next to me and follows his half of the conversation, shaking her head at what she hears and what I can only guess at.

The old man hangs up the phone and turns to her. "He's gone, Christina. They shot him. Five times."

Five times? Jesus, Billy.

Mother's whole body shakes. "Who?" she manages to say, her voice twisted like her throat's not working right

The old man opens and closes his fists. "They don't know. They think it was a robbery."

The robbery I planned.

The old man is breathing hard now, like he's still running up the stairs. "They found him in his office. Shot in the back. He died on the way to the hospital."

Mother leans forward, her arms crossed in front of her stomach like she's going to be sick, and asks again, "Who shot him, Paul? Who?"

The old man shakes his head. "They're still looking," he says.

I sit in the chair, the beer souring in my stomach, my head feeling like it's in a vise, and wonder where the hell Billy is now.

* * *

"It wasn't a robbery," Mother says the next morning, freezing me in the kitchen doorway. For a minute, I think maybe Billy didn't kill him after all.

Outside the kitchen window, the early morning sky has lightened to purple. Mother sits at the table still in her robe, her eyes swollen and circled from crying and lack of sleep. The *Courier-Express* is spread before her. I feel like shit and can't tell if I'm hung over or if it's the guilt eating me.

"What are you talking about?" Father asks from the stove. He holds the coffee pot in one hand, a cup in the other. "Of course it was a robbery."

She shakes her head. "Not according to this."

"It has to be a robbery. What else could it be?" He sets the coffee pot back on the stove and then sits at the kitchen table holding the empty cup.

"There was no sign of a break-in. No broken windows, no kicked-in doors. Nothing." Mother has delicate fingers, the kind that should've plucked harp strings or glided over ivory keyboards, not used to trace the details of a homicide in the morning paper.

"How'd they get in then?" the old man asks, the coffee cup small in his hands.

"An unlocked door."

"Which one? The one from the parking lot?"

Mother shakes her head again. "No. The little one on West Utica. The blue one."

The blue one that doesn't lock right, the one I told Billy about.

Fuck.

"The one to the basement? Who'd leave that unlocked?"

Mother looks up from the paper. "It's been years since I was down in that basement. It's all winding hallways. Somebody must have known their way around pretty well to get in and out of there, especially in the dark."

The chords and tendons are visible in the old man's neck. "Who? A Greek? Ridiculous!"

He stands up, crosses to the kitchen stove, and finally pours his coffee. I grab a box of cereal from the counter and begin to eat directly from it, just to give my shaking hands something to do. The cereal tastes like sawdust.

The old man bangs the coffee pot down on the stove and turns toward Mother like an idea has just smacked him in the forehead. "What was taken?"

"Nothing."

"Nothing?" he repeats. "*Nothing*?"

"Not a thing."

"This can't be," he says in a small voice, the possibility finally taking hold.

I plunge my hand deep into the cereal box. "What's there to steal anyway?" I ask, already knowing the answer.

"What's there to steal?" Father asks, his voice loud again. He holds his cup so tightly I expect it to shatter. "What do you mean, 'What's there to steal'? There's plenty to steal. The collection money. Gold chalices, sterling silver candle holders, the jewels on the Gospel. There's a fortune in that altar."

It's the same list I'd told Billy when he had asked.

* * *

The walk to school is cold. Wind from Canada swirls across the lake and loosens the last grip of summer. I already feel the weight of the layers of clothing I'll wear in the coming months: thermal underwear, heavy sweaters, down-filled parkas.

I walk toward Kenmore West High School, unable to think of anything else but Father George. I try to piece together his last minutes. I knew he had attended the wake of an old Greek; my parents had gone to pay their respects. The funeral parlor is here in Kenmore, so Father George would've traveled south on Delaware Avenue to get back to church. I picture his blue Toyota moving down the street like a scene filmed from a helicopter. The car makes its way through the "S" turns in front of Forest Lawn Cemetery, the headlights knifing through the darkness, before accelerating out of the curves. Father George picks up speed as he heads toward church, only slowing to go around the fountain at Gates Circle. After several more blocks, the right turn signal flashes amber and the Toyota turns into the church's deserted parking lot. He pulls into the spot reserved for him near the side entrance and kills the engine. He gets out of the car, slams the door shut, and heads to the side door. After unlocking it, he makes his way down the hall, past the church office, and enters his study.

Where's Billy? Hiding in the corner? Does Father George turn on the lights? How many steps toward his desk does he take before the shots ring out? Three? Four? And why the hell does Billy shoot him? That was never part of the plan.

I picture Father George sprawled on the floor, the blood soaking through his black suit coat, and I vomit in the bushes near Kenmore West.

Where the fuck did Billy get the gun?

When I straighten, I wipe my mouth with the back of my hand and see my friend McGuire laughing at me along with everyone else who saw me throw up; the girls among them turn away in disgust. Kenmore West, a four-story brick building built during the Thirties as part of the WPA program, looms behind them like a factory. A giant smokestack rises from the roof, but I've never seen smoke come from it. The school looks like it could survive a Soviet blast.

I walk toward McGuire and the rest of the juniors and seniors who are smoking just off school property. McGuire's hair is longer than mine, brushing the tops of his shoulders. He wears faded jeans and a green fatigue jacket. He's growing his first mustache, a ratty thing he constantly strokes like a two-inch pet.

Another kid, one I don't know, stands next to him. His red hair is cropped short and cut around the ears, marking him as a "Joe's Boy", a kid who goes to Saint Joe's, the faggy all-boys high school a few blocks away. He isn't wearing the khaki pants and blue shirt and tie they're required to wear. Instead, he's dressed like me and McGuire in tight Levis and motorcycle boots. He bends forward, cups a match with a freckled hand, and lights a cigarette.

"Still sick from last night?" McGuire asks, grinning at me. He fingers his mustache.

"Fuck you," I say, stopping in front of him. I nod at his cigarette, bumming one without speaking.

He reaches inside his army jacket, pulls out a pack of Camels, and shakes one loose. "You look like shit."

"You seen Billy?"

He digs deep in a pocket designed to hold hand grenades and ammunition and pulls out a plastic lighter. "Not since last night when he dropped us off. He was so wired, we might never see him again." He turns to the red-headed kid. "You'll love, Billy. He's fuckin' nuts. Last night we're in his car and he shoots the "S" turns on Delaware with the lights off, driving totally fucking blind. We must've been going about eighty, sliding from lane to lane, beer spilling everywhere, all of us screaming. Then he comes out of the last turn and pops the lights and we're almost off the fucking road." He shakes his head. "Fuckin' Billy."

He lights my cigarette, still shaking his head, and I inhale and let the smoke fill my lungs and calm my stomach. I blow smoke just past the Joe's Boy's face but close enough to make him blink.

"Who's this?" I ask.

"Fehan. They kicked him out of St. Joe's last week."

"I'm Pete," I say, and shake the freckled kid's hand. We all call each other by our last names, like we're in the army or something. Except for me. My Greek name is too hard to pronounce, so I'm just Pete. Billy isn't Greek, but he's always been just Billy, too, ever since we were kids. His old man used to call him Billy the Kid before he took off.

Jesus.

"So you going?" Fehan asks me.

"Going where?" I ask.

"What the fuck," McGuire says. "Don't you Greeks own a friggin' radio? Haven't you heard?"

The old man had tuned every radio in the house to WBEN, the all-news station, and kept the black-and-white Philco blaring in the front room in case of breaking news about the murder. Even with all that, I still don't know what the fuck they're talking about, so I just shoot twin streams of smoke out my nostrils to show how bored I am with them.

"The Who's coming here," McGuire says. "In December."

"Here?" I ask, looking from McGuire to Fehan then back to McGuire. "You're kidding."

Fehan shakes his head. "They just announced it. We're camping out for tickets to get good seats. You in?"

"In? I'm first in line," I say, but I'm looking past them, hoping to spot Billy on the street.

The warning bell rings, signaling ten minutes until homeroom. Both Fehan and McGuire take final drags on their smokes before flicking their butts at a couple of freshman. They start heading toward school, but I don't move.

"You coming?" McGuire asks over his shoulder.

"No," I answer. "I got to find Billy."

* * *

I walk fast toward Billy's house, the taps on my boots clicking out a warning on the sidewalk. Billy, McGuire's cousin, is already out of school and on his own; he shares a flat with three other guys on the west side. He buys booze for us and sells us weed. Sometimes he lets us hang out at his apartment and listen to albums. I don't have to walk far, though. Billy is waiting for me when I turn the corner from Kenmore West. He's leaning against his car, a black '72 Cutlass. His arms are folded across his chest, a forgotten cigarette burning between his fingers.

He looks worse than I do. His thick, sandy hair is parted in the middle but sticking up in back, like he slept in a chair all night. He's still wearing the same Who T-shirt from the day before, the black one with *The Kids Are Alright* album cover on it, the one where the band is sleeping against a wall with their heads resting on each other's shoulders and a giant Union Jack covering them like a blanket and tucked under their chins. Sunglasses cover Billy's eyes, but I know they must be red and burning, sensitive even to the pale autumn sun.

"Motherfucker," I say, walking right up to him.

"What are you going do? Hit me?" he asks.

Even though I'm in my boots, he still has a couple inches on me and outweighs me by twenty pounds. "What were you thinking?"

"I wasn't thinking anything, Petey Boy," he says, his voice so soft and low I can barely hear it over the passing cars. "You're the thinker, Pete. It was your plan."

"It wasn't a *plan*, Billy. It was us bullshitting around. It was a *game*— which place we could rob and get away with it, like which girls we'd fuck if no one would ever find out. I wasn't serious."

"The cops aren't going to think it was a game, Petey Boy. You're in this as deep as I am."

"You're crazy, man. I'm not in this at all."

"You're not, huh?" He leans close enough for me to smell last night's booze on his breath. "If I get pinched, I'm telling the cops you were with me, that you pulled the trigger."

There's a roaring in my ears, like too much blood is running in the wrong direction. "They won't believe you."

"Only a Greek would know about the blue door with the shitty lock. Or how to get from the basement to the church office."

"Shut up."

"*You'd* know the collection is biggest on the first day of Sunday School when all their parents bring their kids. Not me."

"I wasn't there, asshole."

"No?" Billy jerks a thumb over his shoulder towards the Cutlass. "How many people saw you driving around with me last night? The kids at the arcade, the guy at the beer store, the waitress at the pizza place? How many is that? Eight? Ten witnesses? Maybe more?"

"That was earlier, Billy. Before you shot him."

"Was it? You think a jury won't put the pieces together?"

"My prints aren't on the gun," I say, my mind racing, trying to find a way out of this.

"I'll tell them you wore gloves, Trigger Man."

"Jesus, why are you doing this? What do you want from me?"

Billy sighs then, a long, noisy exhale the way my old man does when he finally gets to the friggin' point. "You gotta help me."

"Help you? How the hell can I help you?"

He notices the cigarette he's holding and looks surprised that it's still between his finger and thumb. He takes a drag, blows smoke out of the corner of his mouth.

"You gotta help me find the gun," he says, his voice breaking for the first time. "I lost it."

* * *

We're driving down Delaware in the Cutlass. Empty beer bottles from last night roll by my feet. This ride is different than when we blindly shot the "S" curves; there's no yelling or laughing, no Who blaring from the 8-track. Entwistle's bass isn't pounding in my chest like a second heartbeat. Billy's not talking much, just killing one cigarette after another. Like my father, he has the radio tuned to the all-news station, but Billy's waiting to hear them say his name. I half expect them to say mine, too, but I know that's just me panicking.

I'm trying not to look scared. The window is rolled down and the cool fall air is rushing over my face and blowing back my hair. The wind is the only thing keeping me from getting sick again. My stomach clenches every time I think about getting arrested, thrown in a cell, and having my face and name all over the papers and TV. The Greeks will have nothing to do with my family if that happens, and it will kill my old man. He's always down at the church for some meeting or another, volunteering for this committee or that fundraiser. If this were back in the old country, they'd run us out of the village and burn our house behind us. Hell, they still might.

Police cars are angled in front of the church and along West Utica. News trucks from all the local channels—WBEN, WGR, WKBW—are parked on the opposite side of the street, narrowing the road so we have to slow down to pass. Billy grips the steering wheel like he's afraid of being yanked out of the Cutlass by his hair. Yellow police tape marked "Crime Scene" cordons off the area in front of the small blue door. A newspaper photographer is snapping shot after shot.

"Jesus, there's cops everywhere," I say, turning in the seat to watch a cop on his knees crawling behind bushes.

"They're looking for the gun," Billy says, checking his rearview mirror to see if anyone is following him.

"How the hell did you lose it?" I ask.

Billy lights a fresh smoke from the butt dangling from his mouth. "I parked a few blocks down so no one would see the car. After I...shot him, I panicked. I just ran. The gun was in my jacket pocket. It must've fallen out. I didn't hear it hit the ground. It must be lying on the grass around here."

He turns on a side street off Utica and pulls to the curb out of sight of the cops. "I parked by that mailbox," he says, pointing. "Let's look from here to there. We can't search for it on Utica, not with all those cops around."

"Jesus, Billy. What if someone recognizes the car from last night? Or thinks it's weird that two guys are crawling around their lawn just a couple blocks away from a murder scene?"

Billy gets out of the car and eases the Cutlass' door closed. "Welcome to my world, Petey Boy."

I get out of the car but don't take a step. Billy is walking with his head down, checking the grass on either side of the sidewalk. He goes about ten feet before he realizes I'm not moving. "What?" he asks.

"Why'd you shoot him?"

Billy just stares.

"Everybody loved that guy. My mom was up all night crying and my old man looks like he's going to explode. Our phone's been ringing off the wall with other Greeks calling and crying. It's like you shot the whole damn Greek community, Billy. It's fucked up."

Billy walks toward me with his head down. He stops a few feet in front of me. When he looks up, his eyes are all red and watery, but I can't tell if that's from chain smoking or if he's about to bawl.

"I pulled the gun and told him to back the fuck off when he walked in on me, but he wouldn't do it. He wasn't even scared. He looked pissed, like he couldn't believe anyone would rob his church. Then he said he was calling the cops. When he turned and reached for the phone, the gun just went off."

"Five times? The gun just went off five times? What the fuck, Billy."

Billy shuts his eyes and sways. "I don't know, man. All the booze and pills and dope. It just happened."

"And for nothing. The paper said nothing was stolen."

"I got something," Billy says, and opens his eyes. "Twenty bucks."

* * *

The whole family is crammed in the front room waiting for the six o'clock news. The room, the smallest in the house, is long and narrow like a shoebox. We're the only family I know who doesn't own a friggin' color TV. Each time I ask the old man about getting one, he tells me he'll buy one when the black-and-white dies. The damn Philco shows no signs of giving out, as if it could go on showing us the world in two colors for another ten or twenty years.

The old man fills the overstuffed chair, a chair too damn large and bulky for the front room but perfect for him. He lowers the paper.

"You're just getting home from school now?" he asks.

I tell him I stayed after to get extra help in math and then hung out with the guys. No one notices the mud on my boots or grass stains on my knees. He opens his mouth to ask another question but stops at the first beats of the snare drums announcing the start of Channel 7's newscast. Fast cut images of the city flash on the screen—City Hall, springtime in Delaware Park, skiers swooshing down snowy slopes, O.J. juking left then right. I imagine the colors: O.J.'s red and blue jersey, the greens and yellows of the park, bright ski vests against a backdrop of white, but all I see is gray.

The murder is the lead story. The same video of the exterior of the church and the parked Toyota are shown again. The anchorman tells us that the police still have no motive, no clues, no weapon.

We couldn't find the gun, either.

"I wish they would stop showing that," the old man says, as we again watch the paramedics pound on Father George's chest. He grips the arms of his chair so tightly his knuckles whiten.

"They showed it at noon, too," Mother says. "And during those news breaks between my shows."

The video of Father George being wheeled to the ambulance ends. The camera is now inside the church, just outside Father George's study; yellow police tape blocks the doorway. The shot zooms in on the blood-stained carpet, the stain wide and expansive. There's more blood than I imagined.

"They can't show that!" Father yells, sitting now on the edge of his chair.

Mother holds a hand to her mouth as the camera focuses on the splattered desk.

Jesus, Billy, I think, and slide down the wall so I'm sitting on the floor. I hug my knees to my chest, wanting to turn away from all that blood, but I can't. On the screen it's black and white, but in my mind it's bright fucking red, so bright it's searing my brain.

The camera cuts to the airport. Father George's wife, *Presveteria* Vicki, had been visiting her family in Cleveland; the reporters are waiting for her when she arrives. Dr. Lambros, our Parish Council president, has his arm around her, trying to console her. Her head rests on his shoulder. She weeps uncontrollably, her whole body shaking. The cameraman must have been kneeling, angling the lens upwards to capture the tears and the way her face twists.

"Poor Vicki," Mother whispers. "Poor, poor Vicki." She pulls the afghan to her chest.

I hadn't thought of Father George's wife, now his widow, or their three kids, all younger than I am. For the first time since I heard my father run up the stairs to tell us about the murder, I feel like crying. It's like those five bullets ripped through Father George's body and hit everybody.

"Look at those reporters," Father says. "Damn vultures."

I'm hoping Billy's mug shot fills the screen next, and at the same time I'm scared that it will. Instead, they run video shot outside the church earlier in the day. A pretty reporter is interviewing a tired looking homicide detective. Thick bags hang under his eyes. He licks his lips and swallows, as if trying to rid his mouth from the taste of cigarettes and coffee. The detective stands a foot taller than the reporter. He tells her that they're considering every angle and following up on all leads, that they haven't ruled out anything yet.

The old man starts to say something in Greek, but the phone rings, cutting him off. I don't move to answer it. I know it'll be another Greek, another person hurting, who just needs contact with someone feeling the same way. My father heads to the kitchen to answer it. I wonder if they call other Greeks or just my old man. They probably think if anyone knows anything, if anyone has any answers, it'll be him.

The phone's still ringing when the doorbell buzzes, and I'm afraid it's Billy wanting to go back and look for the gun again. I get to my feet and open the front door, but it's not Billy wanting to conceal evidence or McGuire wanting to make plans about getting Who tickets. Two men stand on the porch, and I recognize the taller one from the news. Up close the bags under his eyes seem heavier, but the skin coloring is the same shade of gray as it looked on the Philco. My heart starts to pound, like Moonie is smashing it with drumsticks. A weird vibration makes my hands tremble so bad I stuff them in the front pockets of my jeans. I think of all the cop shows I've watched on TV—*Kojak, Baretta, Hawaii Five-O*—and I start hearing "accomplice" bounce around in my head. I expect the detective to reach for the handcuffs, spin me against the wall, and read me my fucking rights.

The tall cop, the one from the news, pulls a gold badge from his suit coat pocket and tells me his name is McCarthy and his partner is Gorski.

Gorski nods. Neither of them smiles. It's like fucking *Dragnet* on my front porch.

I nod back, too stunned to talk, and McCarthy tells me they want to speak to my mother.

"My mother," I repeat, sounding retarded.

Gorski stares at me, taking in my long hair, my grass-stained jeans, the mud-caked boots. I imagine him running my face through mug shots and Wanted posters and I hear Daltrey singing, "*I'm the punk with the stut-ter*".

I step aside and he smiles before squeezing past me into the house. The smile looks unnatural on his face, as if he doesn't use those facial muscles much. Thin lines crease from the corner of his eyes and the sides of his mouth, but they aren't laugh lines. I can't imagine that tall bastard laughing at anything.

"Peter? Who's at the door?" Mother calls from the front room.

"The police," I answer, pushing the words out my dry mouth. "They want to talk to…you."

She walks toward us, taking small steps, as if her legs can't be trusted. She pats the sides of her hair, feeling for forgotten hairclips, and motions the men toward the front room. I'm not sure why she bypasses the larger, more comfortable living room. Maybe she feels safer in the room we use every day. She leads us there and turns off the television.

The detectives sit beside each other on the couch. Gorski pulls a small notebook from his shirt pocket and flips it open. Mother sits engulfed in Father's chair, and I take my place in the doorway, still stunned that two homicide detectives are in my house and that I'm not handcuffed in the back of their Crown Vic.

The old man joins us, summoned by unfamiliar male voices. He stands next to me and I feel small again.

"They're detectives." Mother twists a handkerchief in her lap. "They want to ask me questions."

Father nods at the two men. "Gentlemen," he says, his voice strong and unwavering, as if talking to the police is a daily occurrence for him. "What kind of questions could you have for my wife?"

"Just a few, sir," McCarthy says, and he starts right in, asking us our full names, and Gorski writes down our answers. Then he wants to know about the volunteer work my mother does at the church, but he's not interested in her singing in the choir or baking for the Greek Festival; he wants to hear how she covers the church office on Wednesdays, especially last Wednesday.

"Who else was down there with you?" McCarthy asks, and I swear Gorski is staring at me the whole time, his cop eyes boring into me. I can't even look at him.

Mother turns to the old man for help, but he only shrugs his thick shoulders. None of us knows what the cops want.

She looks back at McCarthy and sighs. "Father George was there and Manny, the accountant, came in to do the books around ten."

"Anybody else?"

Mother rubs her forehead, trying to massage the memory back. "Father George had several appointments. The Morphis girl and her fiancée, Mrs. Tzimas from Greek School...I don't remember the others, but their names would be in the appointment book. Oh, and Frank. Frank was there."

"The custodian?" Gorski asks, without looking up from his scribbling.

"Yes, he was there when I arrived."

"But he didn't work all day, did he, ma'am?" McCarthy asks.

She looks at Father, her eyes widening, as if she had just remembered something horrible. "No."

"Father George fired Frank last Wednesday, didn't he, ma'am?" McCarthy asks.

"No."

Gorski's head jerks up from his pad. "No?"

Mother eyes *Yiayia*'s afghan folded neatly on the couch. I can tell she wants to grab it and cover herself. "Frank quit."

"Why did he quit?"

She folds her hands in her lap, lacing her fingers tightly together. Then she unlaces them and crosses her arms in front of her chest like the old man, leaving the handkerchief on her lap. Mother tells the police that it's a big church with a great deal of wood to polish and carpet to vacuum. There are Sunday School rooms to clean, lawns to cut, sidewalks to shovel, and steps to salt in the winter. Frank told Father George he wasn't being paid enough for all the work he had to do. They argued in the church study, the same room where he was later killed, and Mother had heard it all.

I see where all this is going, and I want to scream at the cops that it wasn't Frank, that it was my friend Billy who pulled the trigger, that I was stoned but home when it happened. But I don't say shit. I just stand there, trying to avoid Gorski's eyes, feeling everything spiral away from me.

"Did Frank threaten Father George when they were arguing?" McCarthy asks.

"He yelled that Father George was always riding him, and Father George yelled that Frank was sloppy and that we were paying him to do the job right. Then Father George said that if he couldn't handle the job, he should quit. So Frank did."

"You didn't hear Frank threaten Father George, ma'am?" McCarthy asks again.

"The yelling was so bad, so ugly, that I left the office. I went to the Ladies Room."

"The accountant said he heard Frank tell Father George to watch his back. You didn't hear him say that, ma'am? That he should watch his back?" McCarthy asks.

Mother sinks way back in the old man's chair, like it's swallowing her. She shakes her head. "I was in the Ladies Room."

I swear to Christ the only sound in the friggin' front room is the ringing in my head. It's so loud I'm sure everyone can hear it, especially Gorski. I can feel his eyes on me without even looking.

"Did they argue a lot before last Wednesday?" McCarthy asks, interrupting the ringing.

Mother shrugs. "Father George wanted his church clean and that's what he expected."

"I see," McCarthy says. "Can you think of anything else that might have happened last Wednesday or recall anything else about the argument?"

Mother shakes her head. She looks drained, like she just did something really hard and is now exhausted.

The detectives exchange looks and stand. Mother rises with them. Gorski slips his notebook back into his shirt pocket.

McCarthy hands Mother his card. "If you think of anything that might help us, please call."

Mother takes the card, her hand shaking, and places it on the arm of the chair, as if the business card were burning her fingertips.

"I'll walk you out, gentlemen," the old man says, and the three of them head for the door.

Mother slumps back in the chair, the color gone from her face. "Peter, get me some water."

When I return, the old man stands with his hand resting on her shoulder. They talk in quiet tones, stopping only when they notice me.

I hand her the glass.

Father pats her shoulder. "At least we know who did it now."

"Frank didn't kill anybody," I say.

"Of course he did," he says, his eyes like storm clouds. "He knew his way around every inch of that church. He could have slipped in and out of there easily in the dark. He could have left that door open or had a key made. He probably even knew Father George's schedule. And now we know why he did it. They'll search his apartment and find the gun and that will be it." He turns away from me, his final point made, the conversation over.

And I still don't say shit about Billy.

"Come," Father says, offering his hand to Mother. "Let's get some coffee. The pot's still warm."

She takes his hand and leans into him as they walk to the kitchen.

I flop down in Father's chair and throw a leg over the arm. My parents' wedding picture stands on one of the end tables. No one will ever call me *Tavros*. From my mother's side, I have inherited the slight build, the thin bones, the narrow shoulders. My face, however, is a carbon of the old man's, especially when he was young. We share the same oval face, the same cleft chin, the identical straight nose. Our faces are mirror images, but that's where similarities end.

The ringing in my head grows louder.

* * *

The next morning, I'm sitting at my desk, forging the old man's signature on a note excusing yesterday's absence, when the phone rings in the hall. I hear the bathroom door unlock and my old man answer it. He talks for a long time, his voice a low grumble. I'm surprised to hear him hang up and knock on my door.

He enters my room shirtless, his skin warehouse white, his stomach soft and loose over the waist of his pajama bottoms. Even his arms and shoulders don't look quite as thick with his shirt off, as if his muscles had shrunk during the night. The towel draped over his right shoulder is smeared with shaving cream; a daub still clings to his earlobe. His hair, rumpled from sleep, looks more silver than I remember, the same color as newly forged tools. He sits on my unmade bed.

"What's wrong?" I ask, turning the note over so he can't see. "You look sick."

"I am sick." He runs his fingers through his hair, rumpling it even more.

"Should I get Mom?"

"No, not that kind of sick."

"Who was on the phone?"

"Mr. Pavlakis."

"So early? What'd he want?"

Father takes a deep breath and looks at me; his face is shaved smooth on one side and dark with whiskers on the other. "I want you to come home right after school today. Don't stay late, not even for Math."

"All right," I say, not knowing what the hell he's getting at. "Why?"

"Get some rest after school. Sleep if you can. Don't eat much. Just something light. Then try to sleep again."

"What's happening?"

He looks at me for the first time. "Threats have been made."

"Threats? What kind of threats? Against who?"

"Father George."

"He's dead," I say, and the old man looks at me like I'm one sorry bastard. His voice is a whisper now, and I have to lean forward to hear.

"His body, Peter. They threatened his body."

He looks at me to see if I've understood, then hisses, "*Desecration.*"

Billy, I think, what the fuck did you do now?

The old man rubs his palms on the top of his thighs as he talks. "The threat was called in to the police. They don't know who it was. Some lunatic, probably."

"What did they say they were going to do?" I ask, none of this really making sense.

He takes several breaths, as if he's pulling the words from deep inside him. His eyes grow bright with tears. I don't remember ever seeing the old man cry, and it scares me.

"Cut him," he says. "His face, his heart."

"Jesus," I say, and slump in my chair.

Why would Billy do that? To throw the cops off his trail? I picture him calling from some corner phone booth, the Cutlass rumbling in neutral at the curb, the cherry pipes sounding angry. I wonder if McGuire is with him, riding shotgun, fingering his mustache and doing one-hitters while he waits for Billy to finish his call.

"The wake will be at the church, not a funeral parlor. There'll be police there guarding him," the old man says, "but the Greeks need to be there, too. The Parish Council and their sons will be sitting in the church around the clock keeping watch. We'll do it in shifts so we're fresh in case something happens. I signed us up from eleven o'clock tonight until seven tomorrow morning. The graveyard shift." His smile is sad, ironic. "That's why you need to rest."

My mouth gapes open, unable to form words. It's all too fucking surreal to be true.

He looks toward my bedroom door. "I need to tell your mother. I don't want her to hear about the threats on the radio or read about it in the papers."

He stands to leave.

"I have plans," I say, the words falling from my lips.

"What kind of plans can you possibly have at eleven o'clock at night?"

"There's a concert. I want to wait in line for tickets with some friends."

I wonder if Billy will be there. I suppose it would look strange if he weren't. I try to picture us—me, Billy, McGuire, Fehan—riding to the concert in the Cutlass like nothing had happened. The car would be smoky with dope and loud from laughter and Townshend's power cords. Somehow I can't see me there.

The old man sits back on the bed. "A concert."

I nod and wait for him to explode, but his voice is dead calm.

"What kind of concert?"

"The Who," I say.

He just stares.

I point to the poster behind him. "Those guys."

He turns and studies the poster of my favorite album cover. I'd bought it from a used-record store just days before. The poster hadn't been for sale; it was part of a display, but I slipped the clerk ten bucks when the owner wasn't there, and he looked the other way when I took it. The poster is an outdoor scene. Blue skies streaked with clouds contrast with the rocky terrain that dominates the shot. The picture was taken right after the band finished pissing against some cement structure; they're zipping their pants, buckling their belts, as they walk away from the wall, the piss stains clearly visible on the cement behind them. Across the top of the poster written in blue is the title of the album: *Who's Next.*

The old man turns to me and gestures over his shoulder with his thumb. "*Those* guys?"

I nod. "Their drummer died last year, so this is probably their last tour, my last chance to see them."

He begins rubbing his eyes with the tips of his fingers, talking while he rubs. "How'd he die?"

I clear my throat, knowing it's going to sound bad even before I say it. "Overdose."

The old man stops rubbing his eyes, leaving them red and watery. He looks at me for what seems like forever. "When I was your age, I dropped out of school to work," he says, starting in on a story I've heard a million times before. "Your *Papou* died and all his responsibilities became mine. Mr. Aleveras hired me as a picker at the tool factory. I've been working there ever since."

The old man looks at the poster behind him again and turns back to me. "You need to start making your own decisions. You're not a baby anymore."

He rolls his head from side to side, as if his thick neck muscles are bunched tight. The numbers flip on my clock radio with an audible click. We both glance at the time.

"I better tell your mother about tonight."

The old man starts for the door, then stops. "Oh, they arrested that bastard Frank," he says. "His fingerprints were all over Father George's office and they found keys to the church that he never turned in. And the sonofabitch doesn't have an alibi, either."

"They don't have the gun," I say, wondering where the hell that piece is, whose jacket pocket it's stuffed in now.

The old man waves at the air like he's swatting my words away. "They have enough without it, but that will turn up, too."

I sit in the chair but don't move, like my ass is bolted to the seat. I stare a long time at the door after my old man closes it behind him. The only sound I hear is my breathing, the numbers flipping on my clock radio, and that damn ringing in my head, like someone is holding a bell to my ear.

* * *

I walk the long way to Kenmore West. I don't want to hang out with McGuire and Fehan and the other smokers this morning. I don't want to talk about the Who and what songs they might play or if we'll get tickets on the floor. The morning news ran video of Frank being taken away in handcuffs, McCarthy and Gorski holding each arm. The image is burned into my brain, and I can't shake it. In the clip, Frank is wearing his Yankees cap, the one he wore when he cleaned the church, and he's yelling at the camera that he didn't do it, that he was home alone watching the Yanks on TV the night Father George was killed. Then the mayor, Jimmy Griffin, fills the screen. He's a little-prick Irishman and doesn't give a shit about anyone except the Irish in the First Ward, his old neighborhood. He's praising McCarthy and what a great job he's done to crack the case so quickly, blabbing on about what a safe city we have and how priest killers will be prosecuted to the full extent of the law. He doesn't mention Gorski, the Polack, at all.

The whole thing makes me sick. I'm still sick as I walk to school. As soon as I saw the mayor I knew Billy was going to get away with it. Old Jimmy Griffin and the cops wanted to arrest somebody, *anybody*, as quickly as possible. Murdered priests are bad for the city, and they want this story off the news and out of the papers right away. I know sure as shit that they'll railroad Frank straight to Attica. There was a guy on the radio this morning already talking about bringing back the death penalty for priest and cop killers; my old man said he'd be the first one to sign that petition, to cast that vote, to pull the damn switch. A hell of a Christian, my old man.

Then part of me thinks that if Billy gets away with it, then I get away with it, too, even if I didn't do anything more than come up with an idea of how to rob the church, an idea I never took seriously. If Frank's convicted, then things will eventually get back to normal for me, for Billy, and for my old man. I won't go to juvie, Billy won't go to jail, and my family won't be shattered and run out of town. And the part of me that's thinking all this shit, the voice that's getting louder in my head and that sounds nothing like my old man's voice, is the part of me that I hate the most.

* * *

By third period I've had enough. The teachers' words are just noise; I haven't taken a single note all morning. McGuire and Fehan aren't in my English class, and I don't see them in the hall between periods. I keep seeing Frank, though, wearing his Yankees cap and yelling at the camera that he didn't shoot anybody. When the bell rings, I blend in with the BOCE kids, the slow ones who go to school for a few hours then get bussed out for vocational training—welding, food service, auto repair. Billy told me once that half the kids in the program end up working the line at Chevy and the other half end up in the Marines catching bullets. Nobody stops me or notices me, and then I'm out the door, around the corner, and gone. I don't even try to be cool. I'm running now, my legs and arms pumping hard, my breath short and gasping from too many smokes. Pain stitches across my right side and down both shins, but I keep running straight to Billy's house.

The Cutlass is parked right out front for everybody to see. It's been washed and waxed since yesterday, the black paint glossy, the chrome gleaming, and it pisses me off. The shiny car looks like a big middle finger, Billy's way of saying that this is the getaway car that nobody saw, that he killed a good man and will get away with it, that some other poor bastard will get twenty-five-to-life instead of him. After I catch my breath, I kick the rear quarter-panel as hard as I can, leaving a good-size dent, my own middle finger to Billy.

I can hear The Who even before I get to the door. It's the part of "Won't Get Fooled Again" where Daltrey gives one of his vocal cord-ripping screams, the kind that hurts the back of my throat every time I hear it. The sound is raw, predatory; it's why Billy likes Daltrey so much.

The door is open. I don't bother knocking; no one would hear it above The Who anyway. The living room is dark except for the weird glow of a lava lamp and the lights on Billy's stereo spiking and dropping with the volume. The sweet smell of hashish hits me. Fehan is sitting on the couch Billy and I garbage-picked a few months ago. He's doing hash under glass. A sewing needle pokes through an album cover with a piece of hash stuck on top. He lights it and covers it with a glass and waits for it to fill with smoke. When it does, he tilts the glass, sucks it empty, and then sinks far back in the cushions.

Billy and McGuire are standing in the corner by the speakers. They're passing back and forth a bottle of George Dickel Tennessee whiskey. The commemorative bottle is shaped like a powder horn from pioneer days. McGuire holds it by the neck and waves it around as he sings along with the music like Davy fucking Crockett at a rock concert. Billy doesn't see me at first, but when he does he lets loose a rebel yell and walks toward me with his arms outstretched. He's still yelling when he wraps me in a bear hug and lifts me off the ground.

When he puts me down, he keeps his arms resting on my shoulders. Our faces are close, his eyes wild and dilated.

"It's over, man!" he yells, above the music. "It's fucking over! They busted someone else. They're not even looking for me anymore."

McGuire lets out his own rebel yell when he hears this and walks towards us.

"He knows?" I ask.

"Hell, yeah, he knows," Billy says. "He's my cousin. Besides, I had to tell him why we're celebrating, didn't I?"

"I can't believe you didn't tell me about the plan," McGuire says, smiling like an idiot. His face is slack from whiskey and dope. He stops in front of us, but his body keeps swaying.

"There wasn't any plan," I yell. "It was just me and Billy talking one night."

"Fuck that," Billy says. "It was a great fuckin' plan. It would've worked, too, if they didn't make the bank deposit right after church."

"And if that priest didn't try to be a fucking hero," McGuire adds, and I want to punch his stupid Irish face. The album side ends and the needle keeps hitting the record label, so a scratching sound comes from the speakers. Fehan's too hashed to get up and flip it.

"What about the gun?" I ask, keeping my voice calm like I'm just making conversation with two old friends. "That may still turn up. Your prints might be on it. You got a record, right? For that Drunk and Disorderly? They got your prints on file, man. They'll match the bullets to the gun and the gun to you."

Billy's face goes a little gray because he knows I'm dead right. "Then we'll just have to find it first, Petey Boy," Billy says, and squeezes my shoulder until it hurts, that scratching and popping sound coming from the speakers the whole time.

* * *

Billy laughs when I tell him I'm not camping out for Who tickets.

"No one's going to cut his body, Pete," he says, grinning, but he never admits to making the threats.

My family, even my *Yiayia*, stops talking to me when I tell them that I won't be standing guard over Father George. My old man doesn't say a word. He doesn't even glare at me when I tell him. I wait for the yelling, the curses in Greek, the listing of reasons why I'm a piece of shit, but I get nothing, just a nod, leaving me to fill out that long list for him.

I'm at the church but not inside with all the other fathers and sons. I'm not sitting in the hard pews with the saints' sad faces staring down at me from the stained glass windows. I'm not sneaking looks at Father George laid out in gold vestments in his coffin in front of the altar, or smelling the stale incense that shrouds the church, or jumping every time the old building creaks, thinking it's some madman breaking in with a knife. I'm not crying.

I'm outside, dressed in black like I'm in a bad movie, crawling around trying to find the gun. I move slowly, looking everywhere, pressing myself into the ground whenever a car goes by, the dew soaking through my clothes. I picture Billy and McGuire and the long line of kids in front of the Central Ticket Office on Delaware Avenue, wrapped in blankets, trying to stay warm, counting down the hours until tickets go on sale in the morning. A hundred different cassette players are probably playing a hundred different Who songs at the same time in a weird jumble of sound. I see and hear it like I'm there, but I'm not.

I cover the same ground, search the same lawns that Billy and I did before and the same ones the cops must've already checked; even in the dark I can see the pressed grass and the footprints of everyone who's covered this area. Time passes, but I don't know how much, and I keep looking, moving slowly, my eyes roving back and forth, my hands feeling in front of me. If I don't find the gun, I'll have to rat Billy out and testify against him. Then he'll tell them it was my plan, that I pulled the trigger, that he only drove. Except for Billy, I've never heard of anyone as deeply fucked as I am.

Then, on a lawn overgrown with ankle-high weeds, I see the gun, the streetlight reflecting off the bluish barrel. The size, the smallness of it, surprises me. I thought something that has done so much damage, hurt so many people, and affected so many families would be a hell of a lot bigger. But it's not. It's a deadly little thing. I wonder if Billy really did wear gloves, if dew wipes out fingerprints, if he'd really pin the murder on me. It would be easy for me to take it and dump it in the river or bury it someplace. It would be even easier just to walk away, to leave it there in the grass for the cops or some other punk to find. I lie there in the weeds not moving, hardly breathing, like I'm the one who's been shot, and stare at that gun a long damn time, trying to figure out what the hell I should do now.

When I finally stand up, I walk the few blocks to the corner of Elmwood and Utica and call the cops from a payphone in front of a bar. The lies come easy. I tell them that while walking my dog, I found a gun not far from where that priest was murdered, that I don't want to be involved, that I'm going to stay anonymous. I give the address where I found the gun and hang up fast. My hand shakes when I light my cigarette. I lean against the wall, the orange neon light of The Elmwood Lounge washing over me, and wait for sirens.

A Person of Interest

Originally published in *Short Story America*

Honan sits in his chair sipping Jameson, the lowball glass lost in his large mottled hand. He stares at the picture of his daughter, Danielle, and his wife, Emily, on the mantle. He'd taken the picture himself the day Danielle graduated from college. Their smiles are identical: broad, unforced, and dimpled. Danielle's blue eyes sparkle as if she'd been looking out on the endless possibilities of her future when the picture was taken. She hadn't seen anything then, of course: not the surprise California trip with her mother as a belated graduation gift, not the hijacking, not the North Tower. Danielle had seen none of those things when Honan pointed the camera at them and told them to smile. She was just smiling for her father, frozen forever at twenty-two.

The glass hovers in front of Honan's lips as he whispers *Mohamed, Waleed, Wail, Abdulaziz,* and *Satam* before taking another sip.

Next to the picture of Emily and Danielle is his framed detective badge, the only evidence in the room of his thirty-five years on the force. It, like the picture frame, is gold.

The doorbell rings and Honan sets his drink down before rising from his chair. His movements are quick and agile for a man of sixty. Getting up early and heading to the gym are all part of the morning routine of his retirement. He opens the door and Michael, his neighbor, stands on the porch, his collar and tie loosened, his sleeves rolled up, facing Mrs. Dougherty's house across the street.

"Michael, this is a nice surprise," Honan says, and means it. He likes Michael. Danielle would've been about his age now. He often wonders what kind of man she would've married, if it would have been someone like Michael with dark eyes and curly hair, if they would've had children, if they would've lived close by.

Michael turns to Honan. "Sam. How've you been?"

Honan shakes his hand. "Good. I was about to watch a ballgame. Want to join me? Have a beer? I could use the company."

"No, I need to talk to you. It's important."

"Sure." Honan steps on the porch. "What's going on?"

"Something happened today. To the girls."

"The girls? Are they all right?"

"They're fine, but Amy's pretty upset."

"What happened?"

"Do you know Mrs. Dougherty's new tenant? Have you met him?'

Honan stares at the house across the street. "Kate rented the flat? When did he move in?"

"I don't know. Yesterday. Maybe this morning."

"I didn't see a U-Haul or hear a moving van. What'd he do?'

"He took pictures of the girls while they were playing out front. He had them smile and pose in all different positions. He took a lot of pictures, Sam."

"He did?"

"I'm sure it's nothing, maybe he's a photographer, but, like I said, Amy's upset. You know, a stranger in the neighborhood, taking pictures of little girls. She's just, just…"

"No, I understand. It's not like it was when Danielle was that age. You just never know nowadays."

"That's what Amy said. She's been calling everyone on the street to see if he's taken pictures of other kids."

"What'd she find out?"

"Nothing, so far. Nobody even knew he moved in, but Amy's got them worried. They're calling and texting people all over the neighborhood about this guy."

"Is that his car?" Honan points to a rusting Plymouth parked on the street, noting the license plate.

"Maybe. Never seen it before."

"Well, let's go talk to him. If it's his car, he's home."

"I don't want to accuse him of anything, Sam. Something like that could ruin a man."

"I understand. We'll just find out what he's up to."

"Maybe I should talk to Mrs. Dougherty first. Maybe she can tell us something about him."

Honan nods. "Katie will know. She always checks her tenants pretty thoroughly before renting to them."

"I think I'll talk to her."

"You mind if I tag along?"

"I was hoping you would."

The two men cross the street lined with old-growth oaks and maples that form a canopy above them. Sunlight filters through shifting and dancing leaves. The houses are sprawling with large front porches, shuttered windows, and wide, green lawns, the kind of homes perfect for large families with laughing children. Kate's house is one of the few rental properties on the block.

An almost forgotten energy tingles through Honan as he climbs Kate's steps. He feels like he has a purpose again, like he's back on the job, about to question a suspect. Once on the porch, Michael presses the top bell three times before the old woman comes downstairs.

"Two gentlemen callers!" Kate says, touching her steel gray hair with an arthritic hand. "What did I do to deserve all this attention?"

"Hi, Kate," Honan says. "I wish this were just a social call, but we may have a problem with your tenant."

"What kind of problem could you possibly have with him? He just moved in." Kate's head twitches involuntarily, and it saddens Honan that her Parkinson's has worsened. They've been neighbors, if not friends, for a long time.

"He's been taking pictures of little girls on the street, Kate. Everyone's pretty upset," Honan says.

"Well, he's only taken pictures of my girls as far as we know, but Sam's right. Amy's beside herself."

"There must be some explanation," Kate says, frowning, the skin around her mouth and neck hanging like crepe paper. "Rahim is an intern at the hospital. All his references said just wonderful things about him."

"Rahim?" Honan asks.

"Rahim Al-Jamil. My tenant."

Honan's body flushes the way it does when he gulps his whiskey. He feels the heat spread through him. "What kind of name is that? Saudi?"

Waleed, Wail, Abdulaziz, and *Satam.*

They were all Saudis.

"I'm not sure. Iraqi, I think. I didn't ask," Kate answers.

This time, the heat doesn't relax him. The muscles in his cheeks quiver. "Let's talk to Rahim," Honan says.

"I just want to find out why he took the pictures, Sam. I don't want to accuse him of anything." Michael turns to Kate. "What's Rahim's last name again?"

"Al-Jamil."

"Amy wants to check the sex offender listing on the Internet to see if he's registered."

"I can check downtown, too. I still have some friends on the force who owe me favors."

"I'm sure he's not on any list," Kate says. "Downtown or otherwise. He doesn't seem that way at all. Not at *all.*"

Honan stabs the lower flat bell with his blunt finger. "Let's find out."

Rahim comes to the door almost immediately. He smiles at Kate, nods at Honan and Michael, and says hello in a quiet voice.

"Rahim, this is Sam and Michael from across the street. Michael lives in the green Victorian and Sam is in the white house. "

"It's a pleasure," Rahim says.

Honan takes in Rahim's slight, almost fragile build, his dark hair, his thin mustache, his ebony eyes. He looks past him into his nearly-empty apartment. "You're not planning on living here long, or hasn't your furniture arrived?"

"I just graduated from medical school. I don't have much."

Michael clears his throat. "Rahim, there's something I wanted to talk to you about."

Honan wrinkles his nose. "What's that smell?"

"Dinner," Rahim answers, then turns to Michael. "What do you wish to talk about?"

Michael shifts his weight.

"Did you take pictures of his girls today?" Honan asks. "Two little blondies playing on the front lawn? About this tall?" Honan sticks his arm out waist high, his palm turned downward.

Rahim nods. "Yes. Yes, I did. You have beautiful girls. They look so happy."

"My wife…"

"Why did you take their picture?" Honan demands.

Rahim takes a step back. "They looked so sweet, so blonde. I sent the pictures to my mother to show her where I live now and how blonde these girls are."

"Your mother?" Michael asks.

"I come from a small village. We do not get blonde visitors there."

"Who else did you send them to?" Honan asks.

"No one. Why would I do that? Just my mother."

"Rahim," Katie says, "can you understand why Michael and his wife are upset? They don't know you and taking pictures of their children makes them wonder about your intentions."

"If you were planning something," Honan adds.

"I meant no harm," Rahim says to Michael. "I apologize if I offended you or worried you. I just thought my mother would like to see the children. I will not take any more pictures of them."

"Damn right," Honan says.

* * *

The next morning, Honan opens his front door to retrieve his newspaper, the taste of soured Jameson still filling his mouth. Sometimes he thinks he only goes to the gym to sweat the whiskey from his system.

As he bends to pick up the paper, he notices Rahim changing the front tire on his Plymouth. Spray-painted in large black letters that run fender-to-fender on the driver's side is the word *PERV*. Honan slips the paper under his arm before crossing the street.

"Looks like you've had trouble," he says.

Rahim turns his head and looks up at Honan. He is dressed in green hospital scrubs, and his thin brown arms seem childlike hanging from the big sleeves. "Yes," he says through his teeth before turning back to the last, frozen lug nut. "I've had trouble."

Honan touches the spray paint with light fingers to see if it's dry. "Doesn't seem like you're making many new friends here, Rahim."

"No," Rahim answers, his arms trembling as he pulls on the lug wrench. The nut doesn't budge. "Not many."

Honan takes a step back, as if reading the graffiti for the first time. "Perv. Is that you, Rahim? Are you a perv? What else do you like doing to little girls besides taking their pictures?"

Rahim ignores him, takes a deep breath, then pulls harder on the wrench.

"Don't want to talk about that? That's fine. I'll find out eventually. Maybe you can tell me what happened to your tire instead. You pick up a nail?"

The wrench slips off the nut and Rahim's knuckles smash into the pavement. He drops the wrench and stands, jamming his bleeding knuckles into his armpits, his face contorting in pain and frustration as he moves away from Honan and the Plymouth.

"Well, look at that," Honan says, squatting in front of the flat tire. "You didn't pick up a nail at all, did you, Rahim?"

Rahim's lips press together.

"Somebody slashed your tire, didn't they?"

"You know they did," he whispers.

Honan eyes the four-inch slice in the sidewall. "Oh, they knew what they were doing, too, Rahim. They slashed you good and deep. Pity, too. Looks like a new tire." Honan looks up at him. "Funny how they always pick the new ones."

Rahim doesn't answer. He sucks a bloody knuckle.

Honan stands, wiping his hands together, brushing off imaginary dirt as if he had tried loosening the nut himself. "You know what I'm thinking, Rahim? I'm thinking this is a sign. I think this slashed tire and spray paint is Allah's way of telling you to find a new place to live, to get the hell out of Dodge. What do you think, Rahim? You think it's time to find a new neighborhood? You think that's what Allah is telling you?"

Rahim takes the knuckle out of his mouth and examines the gash. "I think I'm late for work."

* * *

Michael is standing on Honan's front porch when Honan returns from the gym. His neighbor's black hair is disheveled, as if worried fingers have been running through the locks and pulling at the curls. "I was just leaving you a note."

Honan sets his gym bag down and lifts the front of his gray T-shirt and wipes his face. He drops the shirt, the material darker from the wiped sweat. "Did you see his car?" Honan jerks his thumb over his shoulder. Rahim's car is still parked on the street, the tire still flat, the lug nut still unyielding. The graffiti has been painted over with black primer and the old car now looks abandoned.

Michael nods. "I saw, but something else has happened. You'd better come over."

"What happened?"

"Just come over. Some of the neighbors are there already."

"Can I shower first?

"No, nobody will care. Come on."

Honan follows Michael across the lawn and into his neighbor's house. For decades the Flynns, a couple Honan had always considered old, had lived in this house. Honan is now the same age as they were when he first moved next door. He and Emily had spent countless nights in their formal living room filled with Victorian furniture, handmade lace doilies, and Martha's Baby Grand. Now when he comes over, the brightly painted walls, the flat-screen television, and the strewn children's toys make him feel as if he has never set foot in this house before. Amy hugs him and kisses him on the cheek.

"Thank you for coming," she says. She wears no makeup and her skin is pale but darker under her eyes. Her hair is a shade lighter than Danielle's but about the same length as in her graduation picture. Honan wonders if the two women would've been friends, if their children would've played together, if Danielle would've painted her own living room as brightly.

The house is filled with neighbors. They stand or sit in couples, whispering to themselves or others, huddling close to each other. There is no laughter, just the occasional weak smile. Honan recognizes faces he's seen cutting lawns and walking dogs, but he knows few names. The only other old-timer there is Kate Dougherty, who sits in a straight-back chair by the unlit fireplace. The rest are part of the new wave of neighbors, like Michael and Amy, who bought houses from Honan's friends and moved in with young families and SUVs. He never imagined that he'd be living alone and surrounded by strangers.

"Everyone," Michael says. "Sam's here. Does everyone know Sam Honan from next door? Sam's a retired police officer and I thought it would be a good idea to hear his opinion."

Honan nods to the people who smile thin smiles and nod at him. "You said something new happened, Michael?"

"Yes," a woman with short red hair and thick glasses answers. Honan guesses she's not much past thirty. "I'm Pat Walker and this is my husband Bob." She puts her hand on the shoulder of the balding man standing next to her. He nods at Honan.

"We live in the yellow house on the corner."

Honan nods back. The Sanders's old house. He remembers their Christmas parties—the large spruce decorated in the parlor, the caroling, Emily in her Christmas sweater. "Something happened at your house, Pat?" he asks, pushing the memories away.

She nods. "Some of my daughter's clothes were…stolen. And then when Amy called and told me about her girls…." Her voice breaks, and her husband puts his arm around her shoulder, pulling her close. "She's only six."

"Somebody broke in?" Honan asks. "Did you call the police?"

She shakes her head. "It was such a nice day, I decided to hang clothes out to dry. I like to do that sometimes. I know it's old fashioned, but my mother used to, and I…."

"I understand," Honan says, remembering how Emily would hang clothes to dry and how their sheets would smell like crisp air. He knows if he hung them on the line now the scent would only remind him why his bed is half empty.

"They were stolen from the backyard?" Honan asks.

Pat nods. "A purple top and matching shorts." Her face collapses, scrunching together. "And three pairs of panties. Why would anyone steal a little girl's panties?"

"Her teddy bear is missing, too," her husband adds.

The other couples murmur to each other and shake their heads, although they already know this news. Those who are close reach out to rub Pat's arm and squeeze her hand.

"Sam, what can we do about this?" Michael asks. "It feels like it's escalating already. I can sense it."

Honan rubs his hand across his chin and mouth; his whiskers whisper against his palm. "You need to call the police and report this, if you haven't already. They aren't going to go door-to-door looking for stolen clothes, but we need to get this on record. The same thing with the picture taking, Michael. He didn't break any laws by photographing your girls, but the police need to know about it."

"So you think it's Rahim then?" Bob Walker asks, his arm still around his wife.

"I do," Honan answers. "None of this started happening until he moved in. I've lived on this street longer than anybody but Kate, and we never had any trouble like this before. Never."

"It all circumstantial, Sam, and you know it," Kate Dougherty says, her head twitching but her voice strong. "Whatever happened to innocent until proven guilty?"

"I didn't say we could convict him, Kate, but he's the one. I'm sure of it. We need the police to be aware of all this circumstantial evidence so they'll consider him a person of interest and start investigating." Honan turns to Amy. "Did you check the sex offender registry?"

"I did. The local and national one. He's not on either."

Honan nods, as if this news doesn't surprise him. "I had a friend run his plate. He's clean. No record for anything, not even jay walking."

"That's because he's a decent person, Sam," Kate says. "Everyone who knows him says so. He's going to be a doctor."

"He's going to be a doctor, all right. I checked on that, too. Do you know what his specialty is, Kate? Pediatrics. Do you know what kind of careers pedophiles choose? They choose jobs that give them access to children: teachers, priests, counselors, coaches, and *pediatricians*. It's the same reason he chose to live in a neighborhood full of families. I guarantee you he picked this street because of all the little kids who live here. Your little kids," Honan says, looking around the room, staring into each set of eyes he meets.

The living room is quiet for a moment, and then everyone begins talking at once, drowning out Kate's voice. Concern is replaced with anger and frustration. The neighbors look around the room with glaring eyes and hard-set faces.

"So what do we do, Sam?" Michael asks. "How do we stop this guy?"

"We can't just sit around and wait until he attacks one of our kids," Bob Walker says.

"It's just a matter of time before he strikes. He's just waiting for the opportunity," his wife adds.

"I've already talked to him about moving out," Honan says.

"You did not!" Kate Dougherty rises unsteadily from her chair.

"I did. I told him this wasn't the neighborhood for him and he should move on."

"You better not have touched that boy's car, Sam Honan," Kate says, pointing a shaking finger at him. "He has practically nothing, only that car and some boxes."

"I only talked to him, Kate. And it looks like I'll have to talk to him again."

* * *

Two police cars are already in front of Kate's house when Honan comes out the next morning. The officers are standing near the Plymouth taking Rahim's statement. The front tire remains flat, but "9-11" is freshly spray-painted in white over the black primer; "PERV" is spray-painted on the trunk in dripping letters. Rahim points to Honan, and the officers turn to look at him. The older officer nods and walks across the street toward Honan, who waits for him with his arms crossed and his legs wide.

"Morning, Sam," the sergeant says, and extends his hand.

Honan grips the officer's hand. "Phil, it's been a long time."

"You're looking good. Retirement must be agreeing with you."

"You're lying, and judging from all that gray hair, you'll be finding out about retirement soon enough."

Phil laughs and smoothes his salt-and-pepper hair with his palm.

Honan raises his head and gestures across the street with his chin. "It looks like my new neighbor has had more trouble."

The officer looks at the vandalized car. "Yeah, it sure does." He turns back to Honan. "He seems to think you had something to do with it."

Honan shakes his head. "Not me. He has all the dads riled up in the neighborhood. It could've been anybody. This guy is bad news, Phil. They want his blood."

Phil nods. "I read the reports your neighbors filed yesterday. We'll keep an eye on him. You know how it works. But it's different now."

"Different?"

"Spray painting '9-11' on his car changes everything. This will get flagged as a hate crime and will be sent to a special unit to investigate. The mayor appointed them himself. They're not one of us, Sam. They're all new guys, outsiders. They don't remember you or know your story. They'll treat this like any other hate crime investigation."

Honan points to the Plymouth. "*That's* a hate crime?"

Mohammed, Waleed, Wail, Abdulaziz, and *Satam*

"It is. You need to watch yourself, Sam. I'm telling you this as a friend."

Honan snorts and shakes his head. "I'll spread the word to the other dads. I'll tell them to cool it and let the police do their job."

"I don't want to come back here, Sam. You hear what I'm saying?"

"I hear you, Phil, but it's always so good to see you."

* * *

Caught somewhere in that filmy grayness between sleep and awareness, Honan wakes from his nap disoriented and unsure of his location. It's not until he settles on the picture of Danielle and Emily that he realizes where he is and why the house is so quiet. He sits up on the couch and his head throbs from the movement. His fingertips lightly massage his temples as he leans forward and rests his elbows on his thighs. The bottle of Irish whiskey and his glass wait for him on the coffee table, but he ignores both. He rises and takes unsteady steps to the mantle and stares at the photograph. If he shuts his eyes, he can still visualize every detail—the tassel strands, the angle of Danielle's mortarboard, the laughter in Emily's smile. He glances into the mirror above the fireplace and stares into his own red-rimmed eyes. The dark half-moons beneath them contrast with the pale skin devoid of the ruddiness he'd had when he was younger, when Danielle and Emily were still alive.

Movement outside his front window catches his attention, and Honan moves away from the mantle and pushes aside Emily's sheer curtains. Across the street, Rahim loads a box into the backseat of the Plymouth before turning and disappearing into his apartment. The slashed tire has been replaced with a mismatched blackwall. Once again, the graffiti covering the car has been covered with primer. The Plymouth's large trunk is open and gaping. Rahim reappears in his doorway, straining as he carries a heavy carton. The bottom gives way and books spill onto the walk. Honan slips into his shoes and heads out the door, ignoring his throbbing head. Rahim is still on his knees, repacking the books, when Honan reaches him. He reads some of the titles—*Textbook of Pediatric Emergency Medicine, Pediatric Cardiology for Practitioners, Critical Care Techniques*—before Rahim shoves them in the carton.

"Going somewhere, Rahim? You're not leaving our friendly little street, are you?"

Rahim glares at him. "Yes, you've gotten your wish. I'll be gone in the morning."

"I'm glad my little talk earlier convinced you."

Rahim rises to a crouch and slips his arms under the box, support-
ing the bottom as best he can. He walks bent forward, his back rounded,
his thin arms shaking, and loads the ruptured carton into the trunk
already half-filled with boxes and bags.

He straightens, places his palms on the small of his back, and pushes his slender hips forward. "Your talk had nothing to do with this. Your
words are meaningless to me, just noise from a bitter old man. Mrs.
Dougherty convinced me that it would be best for me to leave."

Honan's eyebrows arch. "Kate? She's the only one who didn't want to
run you out of town this morning."

"She told me of your meeting, of all the anger in the room, and how
she is afraid for me. She said my car was only the beginning and that I
was in danger, and I believe her. Mrs. Dougherty is very kind. She gave
me my money back. The security deposit, the first and last month's rent,
all of it. When my friends return to town in the morning, I will stay with
them until I find another apartment far from this neighborhood."

"I've known Katie a long time. She's a smart woman, but you sure
got her fooled."

"I did none of those things you accuse me of. I don't know anything
about stolen clothes or missing teddy bears. I only took pictures to send
to my mother."

"Well, that doesn't even matter now. The important thing is that
you're leaving."

"Yes, I hope you are satisfied."

Honan's smile is forced and unnatural. He doesn't feel satisfied at all.

* * *

The smell of smoke brings the neighbors to their porches and to
the foot of their driveways. They stand in their pajamas and robes, arms
around each other, holding each other close, watching the Plymouth
burn in the night. No one moves to help as Rahim runs from the back

of Kate's house with a garden hose. Everything he owns is boxed and bagged in the car that's now being licked by growing tongues of orange and yellow flame. The hose is kinked somewhere and the water only trickles. He runs back up the driveway to straighten the hose as the Plymouth burns and burns and burns.

Honan leans on his porch rail and watches the fire intensify. In the distance, a siren cries. He wonders if the pumper will arrive before the gas tank explodes, if the trees above the car with their dancing leaves will catch fire, if his neighbor's windows will shatter. The heat from the car reaches him, and he feels it hot on his face, drying his eyes. He turns away. Shadows from the flames flicker across his house, as if his home is being consumed by the same fire that's not only destroying all of Rahim's possessions, but all that Honan has left as well. He takes a step inside the house, unable to look at Emily's picture. When he raises his glass, his hand smells of Irish whiskey and gasoline. He drinks deeply and waits for the explosion, for the satisfaction. Neither comes, and the siren grows louder.

The Luckiest Man in the World

Originally published in *Aethlon*

I t was Big Sugar's idea to auction off my grandfather's baseball. He whispered the idea from behind the bar, his voice a leathery rasp as it has been since a throat punch ended his boxing career.

"What do you know about auctions?" I asked, after taking a small sip of my beer, hoping he'd buy me one on the house soon.

He leaned his great brown head nearer to me, a habit he'd developed so people could hear his soft voice above noisy crowds. Some of the old timers said he talked like he'd boxed, leading with his face.

"That's where I get my stuff," he said, and nodded to the boxing memorabilia decorating the bar. The walls were lined with fight posters and photos: a black and white of Jimmy Slattery, his bare fists raised, his Irish chin up, daring the camera; a "Bash in Buffalo" poster from when Roberto Duran fought Biglen downtown at the old auditorium. My favorite pictures hang by the jukebox, framed photos of fighters with big hearts to go with their hard hands—Lamotta, Bobby Czyz, Boom Boom Mancini before he killed that Korean—guys I'd tried to copy when I used to fight.

Mixed in with the greats were photos of Big Sugar from his fight days, most taken when he was young and his face still smooth and his right eye-lid opened all the way, before he started forgetting drink orders—Sugar as a teenager, winning the Golden Gloves in Albany; another from his first pro fight against that Puerto Rican southpaw who ended up in Attica; a picture of Big Sugar and Ali taken at some hotel lobby in Atlantic City. Sugar's smile was wide, like a kid's. Ali's face was a Parkinson mask.

"You got all that stuff at the auction?" I asked.

Big Sugar nodded. "Except the ones of me."

"I was gonna take the ball to that place on Hertel Avenue," I said. "See how much he'd give me for it and then decide."

Sugar shook his head like he was shaking off an eight count. "He'll rip you off, man. He'll turn around and sell it and triple his money. I'm telling ya, Paulie, the auction is the way to go. You'll get more money for it that way."

"How much more?"

Sugar shrugged as he shuffled down the bar to wait on another customer. "Beats me. I don't know shit about baseball."

I stared at my hands, the knuckles battered and deformed, my ring finger pointing off at an angle. On cold days when they ache and the joints lock, it takes both hands to hold the baseball signed by every member of the 1946 New York Yankees—DiMaggio, Rizzuto, Dickey, all of them. Yogi Berra was a rookie in 1946 and signed the ball "Lawrence Berra". That alone had to make it worth something. Joe McCarthy, the Yankees manager at the time, was driving through town in the winter of 1946 when he pulled into my grandfather's garage in his backfiring Cadillac Sedanette. They talked baseball while Papa Nick fixed the Caddy. When my grandfather got the engine running smooth again, McCarthy popped the trunk and handed him the ball before paying him and driving off. Papa Nick loved the Yankees and loved that ball; he kept it in a clear plastic cover to protect it. Sometimes I would tease the old man, remind him that the 1946 Yankees were an awful team, finishing seventeen games behind the Red Sox, but he didn't care. According to him, after Christ and FDR, DiMaggio was the greatest person who had ever lived. "And remember," he would always say, lowering his voice so my grandmother wouldn't hear, "Christ never played centerfield."

When the old man died, he left me the ball, which surprised everyone, especially my brother Dean. He was the one who liked baseball, not me. Baseball was boring. There was too much standing around and waiting for something to happen, but I'd liked boxing from the first time I walked into Singer's Gym on Main and Chippewa and smelled the sweat and heard the speed bag's rhythm and the duller thud of someone working the heavy bag. Even towards the end when I knew I was done, I liked the way my hands trembled from fear and adrenalin when they were getting taped before a fight. It took courage to bend between the ropes and go into the ring; it took more courage to get off the canvas when the black lights were exploding in my head and I couldn't tell whose blood was splattered on me, mine or the other guy's. It's the only sport where you're physically punished for your mistakes.

But I had liked spending time with Papa Nick and hearing his stories of the Old Country, or the old days, or of DiMaggio, so I'd go to his house and lie on the couch with ice packs on my ribs or a bag of frozen peas on my eye and listen to him while a ballgame flickered on the television.

I was surprised when Dean slid on the stool next to me. Sugar frowned when he saw my brother; he hasn't liked him since Dean bet against me on the Ramirez fight. Dean knows it and doesn't come around much. He raised his hand anyway, signaling Big Sugar for a beer.

My brother turned to me then, his face ballplayer smooth, no scars across his eyebrows, his nose still straight, his teeth unchipped. "I heard you're selling the ball."

"Where'd you hear that?"

"Jackie told Marcy."

Wives. I wondered what else my wife had said.

Sugar put a beer in front of both of us and then stood back, folding his thick arms across his chest, and stared at Dean. After all the years, after all the fights, even with all the blows to the head, Big Sugar was still a dangerous man.

"So why you selling it?" Dean asked, ignoring Sugar.

"I'm only thinking about selling it. I haven't decided anything."

"So why are you thinking about selling it?"

"I need money."

"Then you shouldn't have quit your job. That was a good gig I got you at the warehouse. Lou did a personal favor for me bringing you on."

"I couldn't take the cold, Dean. In and out of the refrigerated part of the warehouse on that forklift was killing me. After twenty minutes, my hands would start screaming. After an hour, I couldn't move them."

"A non-union job like that doesn't come along every day."

"I know."

He shook his head, disgusted with me, sipped his beer, and then shook his head again. Big Sugar kept looking at him, his eyelid drooping more the longer he stared.

"So sell me the ball. You know I've always wanted it. It'll stay in the family that way. Papa Nick would've wanted that."

I took a long pull on my beer so I wouldn't have to answer right away. If I were going to sell it, it would make sense to sell to him. Dean does pretty well in the insurance game. He and Marcy have a nice three-bedroom out on in the suburbs and a little girl who inherited his straight nose.

"Look, I'll give you five hundred for it right now. I got the money with me."

I nodded and took another long swallow. Dean once told me that when somebody hesitates about signing a life insurance policy, he'll make his eyes and voice go soft and he'll whisper to the guy, "Don't you think your family will need this insurance money if—God forbid—something happens to you? Do you think you're the luckiest man in the world and nothing could possibly happen?" Then he'll push the pen across the table to the poor guy who's now thinking about car crashes and cancer.

Dean's eyes were soft looking when he offered me the five hundred. Big Sugar shook his big head.

"What?" Dean turned to me, then to Big Sugar, and then back to me. "This guy's your financial advisor now? You just said you needed money. Hell, Jackie told Marcy the same thing this morning."

"I might auction off the ball."

"Auction?" Dean sat straighter on his stool. "What auction?"

I looked to Big Sugar for help. I knew as much about auctions as Sugar did about baseball. He leaned closer to Dean. "There's an auction house on Cazenovia Street."

Dean made a face like his beer tasted bad. "Cazenovia Street? *South Buffalo*? There's no auction house in South Buffalo. Hell, there's nothing down there but Irish bars and unemployment."

Sugar's voice remained low and steady. "There's an auction house right off Seneca Street. Used to be a Masonic Temple except all the Masons started dying off and the ones that were left sold the building. The new owners run auctions there the first and third Tuesday of every month now. Rest of the time they rent out the rooms for weddings and parties and such."

"I fought there as a kid," I said, remembering the big brick building with the columns out front that looked like it could survive a nuclear blast. "The Masons would set up a ring in the hall downstairs and cheer like hell when we started beating on each other."

"That's the place," Sugar said, nodding. "They hold the auctions in that same room. Got a full kitchen and bar in back."

"What do they auction off down there?" Dean asked. "GED certificates and home pregnancy tests?"

Sugar's good eye closed a bit so the lid was almost even with the droopy one, and I imagined him uncrossing his arms and flicking his jab again, catching Dean right in the mouth and knocking him off his stool, his beer flying one way, his front teeth another.

Sugar kept his arms folded. "They auction off all kinds of shit. Antiques. Furniture. Books."

"And baseballs," I said, not knowing if they'd ever auctioned a single ball.

Dean sighed then and looked over both shoulders like he expected muggers by the jukebox or sneaking out of the men's room. He pulled an envelope from his sport coat and slapped it down on the bar. He didn't have to tell me what was inside.

"There's five hundred dollars in there," he said, pushing it toward me with his fingertips. "Five hundred. That's a month's rent or a couple car payments. Hell, maybe you can get your hands fixed with that."

Jackie must not have said anything about the pregnancy or Dean would've added doctor bills and diapers to the list. I'm glad she didn't. We made a deal this time that we wouldn't tell anyone until long after the first trimester, just in case we lost this one, too.

"Cost a lot more than five hundred to get his hands fixed," Sugar said, scowling like he was the one who'd been insulted.

"To be honest, Dean," I said, pushing the envelope back toward him, "I'm not sure what the ball's worth. I never looked into it. I never thought I'd sell it."

He looked at me like I'd taken too many head shots. "You're going to sell the ball and you don't even know what it's worth?" He slapped the bar with both hands and leaned back on his stool. "Unbelievable."

Sugar bent real close this time. "At an auction, there might be three or four guys there like you with envelopes in their pockets, and the price just goes up and up." Sugar reached out with a crooked finger and opened Dean's jacket. "How many envelopes you got in there?"

Dean slapped Sugar's hand away, not hard, though. He knew better. "I gotta hit the head," he said, and slid off the barstool. He grabbed the envelope before heading to the men's room. Sugar gave me a disgusted look like I had picked Dean to be my brother.

I went over to the jukebox before Sugar could start telling me what he thought of him; I'd heard that sermon too many times since the Ramirez fight, the fight I lost and Dean won big; I never knew how much he won betting against me, probably a couple grand, maybe more.

While a song played that I hadn't selected, I studied the pictures by the jukebox; there's one of me there. My voice had been almost as soft as Sugar's when I'd asked if he'd hang it near the ones of Mancini and LaMotta. I don't remember who took the photo or how I got it. It's a five-by-seven and not even in color, so it has an old-time look to it, like I had fought decades earlier. It was taken between rounds. I'm sitting on the stool in my corner, my body hard looking, the sweat coating my shoulders and chest, reflecting the camera's flash. I'm leaning forward, my arms resting on my thighs, my gloves touching, glaring across the ring at whomever I was fighting. My muscles are tense and bulging, like I can't wait for the round to start; there's not an ounce of fat on me. Maybe I'm twenty in the photo, twenty-two tops, and I have that hungry, naïve look of youth that says I can't be beaten, that everything's still possible. Some days now, when my hand is feeling good, I want to punch that photo with all I got left and shatter the glass so the shards slice the picture in a hundred places.

When Dean came out of the bathroom, he waved me back to my stool and switched us from beer to double Dewars and started a tab. Two or three drinks later his offer on the ball went up to fifteen hundred, and I had a feeling he knew exactly how much that ball was worth.

"That's a hell of deal I'm giving you," he said, his eyes and lips wet. "A hell of a deal. You're lucky to get a deal like that. And you know why? Because you're family. Family takes care of family, right? Isn't that what Papa Nick always said?"

I nodded, my head fuzzy from the booze, and thought of the warehouse job he'd gotten me, how my hands would turn into frozen claws, and how his buddy Lou had always called me Meat and never by my name. I wonder what Papa Nick would've thought about that.

"Fifteen hundred for a ball signed by a third-place team. A *third*-place team, you lucky son-of-a-bitch," he said, and gulped more scotch.

The door opened then and a pretty young Latina, barely drinking age, walked in alone. Everything about her was big: her black hair was piled high; silver hoops, the size of handcuffs, dangled from her ear-lobes; she must have been about six feet in those heels. I'd seen her be-fore, but I couldn't remember where.

Dean spun on his stool to face her and said, "Sweet Jesus" loud enough for her to hear. The corners of her mouth curled just a bit.

"She's young, Dean," I said.

"She's old enough," he answered, and was off the stool and moving to the corner table where she was headed. I'd stopped reminding him years ago that he was married.

"That's trouble in heels," Sugar whispered, sliding a glass of ice wa-ter in front of me that I didn't ask for.

"Dean can take care of himself."

"That's the only one he ever looks out for," Sugar said. He reached for the remote by the cash register, flicked on the television behind the bar, then flipped channels until he landed on a ballgame.

The Yankees were wearing pinstripes, so I knew they were playing at home. I usually think about Papa Nick when a game comes on, es-pecially if the Yankees are playing, but I probably would've thought of the old man if Sugar had turned on a soap opera. He had been in my thoughts constantly since Jackie had told me the baby news and asked what we were going to do for money now that I wasn't working. For days now, I'd been arguing with myself about selling the ball, going back and forth, beating myself up with guilt about it. Even though I was no base-ball fan, I thought Papa Nick had left me the ball because he thought I'd hang onto it, keep it safe, and tell the story to my kids and grandkids about the time the great Joe McCarthy drove into his garage in a mis-firing Cadillac. He knew that if he left Dean the ball, he would've taken the first good offer he got, and I bet it would've been more than fifteen hundred.

As I sipped the ice water, not really watching the game, I thought of what Dean had said about family. Papa Nick talked about it all the time, especially when he was telling stories about the Depression and how various family members moved in with them. They all shared what little they had—clothes, food, money—and somehow they got through it together. Maybe it was the booze or maybe I was just trying to convince myself, but suddenly I thought that Papa Nick would be okay with me auctioning the ball and I shouldn't feel guilty about it. That maybe the ball had sat in its plastic case on my dresser long enough and it was time for it to help my family get through a tough time.

"Here we go," Big Sugar said, and I glanced up at the TV, thinking something was going on in the game, but Sugar was looking past me to the door.

I turned and saw Hector, a featherweight who trained out of a gym on Niagara Street, standing in the doorway. He was staring hard at the corner table, his fists clenching and unclenching by his sides, and I remembered where I had seen the Latina: with him. It's funny how those little guys always hook up with big women. Hector and her were similar though, both all flash and wanting attention. Strings of gold chains drooped from his neck, and he wore heavy rings on almost every finger. He was a pretty good fighter, though, with fast hands and a killer's sense of how to finish when he had someone hurt.

I looked to the corner then, too, and saw Dean stroking the Latina's arm. They were leaning over the table toward each other, and Dean was whispering something in her ear. She was smiling. He had to kiss her cheek then.

At that instant, like a gypsy fortune teller, I saw how the next few minutes would play out, like how sometimes in the ring I'd know what punch would be thrown before my opponent snapped it, giving me time to duck, or cover, or counter. Hector's body would tighten, his face would grow darker, his voice would erupt in Spanish. He'd move toward the table, featherweight quick, knocking chairs out of his way, tossing the table on its side to get to Dean. The Latina would scream and shrink back, trying to get the hell out of the way of the violence that was coming. Then Dean would either stand or be pulled to his feet and Hector's fast hands would start flying in combinations, his heavy rings digging into my brother's unmarked, ballplayer face.

I looked over at Sugar behind the bar; he was watching them and knew what was about to happen, too. His arms were crossed and there was a mean light dancing in his good eye. He was smiling, waiting, and I knew he wouldn't stop it or break it up. Dean had been running up a tab for years, and Sugar wanted to see it finally paid.

Then, before I even knew what I was doing, I was off my stool, moving toward the corner, loosening my neck muscles, the almost forgotten feeling of strength coursing through me as I heard Papa Nick echoing in my ear. Hector was young and quick, but he was angry and I wasn't. I could still take punches, roll with them, and then throw my own with bad intentions when I had to. I knew later, after it was over, after I got my brother out of there in one piece and got myself home, how much I would hurt and how Jackie would take my broken hands in hers, hold them to her face, and wet them with her tears.

The Aerialist

Originally published in *Pulp Modern*

Blind Charlie wanted to see the Frenchman fall. He looked at Spence above the newspaper, his eyes distorted through thick lenses. "I bet you twenty bucks he hits the street."

Spence put down his racing form and glanced at the rows of television screens mounted near the Off Track Betting Parlor's ceiling. Live feeds from racetracks across the country—Indiana Downs, Chester, Pimlico—were being broadcast. "How high will he be?"

"Twenty-three stories. He's walking between the replicas of the Statue of Liberty at either end of the Liberty Building."

Spence pictured the building at the corner of Main and Court. It was one of his favorites. He had always liked how the statues were illuminated at night, their torches blinking as a warning to low-flying aircraft. When he was lost downtown, confused by the one-way streets, he'd look for the Liberty Building to regain his bearings.

"It's not really twenty-three stories," he said.

Blind Charlie's eyes raced side-to-side behind his coke-bottle glasses. "Yeah, it is. It says so right here." He raised the newspaper as proof.

Spence shook his head. "If he's walking between the statues that means he's above the roof. That's only got to be two stories, maybe three. He'd never hit the street if he fell. Just the roof."

Blind Charlie frowned at this, a ridge forming between his eyebrows the way it does when sure things finish out of the money. Spence took the newspaper from his hands and started reading the article about the French aerialist.

Didier Pasquette planned to walk one hundred and fifty feet between the east- and west-facing statues across a steel wire as wide as his thumb as the kickoff to a week-long art festival. Spence didn't know what walking across a high wire had to do with art, except that the Frenchman's costume, hand-painted by German artist Kai Althoff, would be on display all week at the Albright-Knox Art Gallery if he didn't fall. There would be no safety harness, no net, nothing to save him if he made a misstep. Pasquette's walk promised to be the greatest aerial exhibition in Western New York since the Great Farini crossed the Niagara Gorge in 1860 with a wooden washing machine strapped to his back. Spence thought Farini's walk above the rapids and rocks had been far more dangerous than Pasquette's intended stunt. He was certain that Farini must have used a real rope back then, rope that could fray with knots that could fail, not one made out of twisted steel that could hoist a Buick. If Spence had lived back then, he would have bet against Farini.

"Maybe," Blind Charlie started, the ridge between his eyes even more pronounced now. "Maybe if something goes wrong, really wrong, he'd miss the roof. Then he's falling twenty-five, maybe twenty-six stories, and not just two or three before he hits."

Spence put down the paper. "Maybe." He glanced at the wall clock. It was almost post time for the first race at Monticello. He wondered who N. De Souza was, the jockey riding Two Steppin' Tango at 10-to-1 in the first; if he was related to the great Brazilian jockey Silvestre De Souza; if talent and luck ran in the family. Spence filled out the worksheet, betting two bucks that Two Steppin' Tango, the number five horse, would show. He hoped the white pages in Sao Paulo didn't contain columns of De Souza's.

"You betting?" Spence asked, pushing back his chair from the table and rising.

"What about wind?" Blind Charlie asked, pulling the newspaper back to himself and holding it close to his failing eyes. "It's got to be windy twenty-five stories up, right? Gusty? That could blow him over the side."

Spence shrugged and headed to the mutuel windows to place his bets. There was a line at Sylvie's cage, but Spence got in her queue anyway, like he always did. He told the regulars who noticed that there was nothing to it, that he was just superstitious, that placing bets with Charlie's wife brought him luck. The OTB people nodded and said nothing more about it, fully understanding the power of rituals and jinxes. Sylvie caught his eye above the heads and shoulders of the white-haired men in front of him, old retirees twice his age who made up the usual afternoon betting crowd, and smiled. Spence smiled back, feeling his face warm. She had large, straight teeth, and when she gave him a full smile like she had just now, brightening her eyes and face, it was like she had turned on the high beams just for him.

The line and distance gave Spence the opportunity to watch her as she sat balanced on her stool, entering wagers. She was still tan even though it was late September, and her brown skin contrasted with her white teeth, making the smile she'd given him appear even brighter. Her hair, highlighted blonde from the sun, hung loose to her shoulders and not pulled back like she usually wore it at work. Spence thought he could stand there all day and just watch her.

Each of the men in front of Spence, men old enough to be Sylvie's father, took their time placing their bets and tried to flirt with her; Spence heard them calling her sweetie and hon like they had a shot. She would smile at them but just with her lips and not with her eyes at all. Spence shifted his weight from one leg to the other, looked at his bare wrist out of habit, his watch, he hoped, still at the pawnshop on Broadway. He glanced at the wall clock again.

When Spence finally reached the head of the line, he placed his bet, speaking clearly the name of the track, the race number, the two-dollar minimum wager on Two Steppin' Tango. He relaxed only when he was sure he had gotten his bet in on time. He was last in line. The others, their wagers already placed, had crowded beneath the monitors to watch the race from Monticello, all except Blind Charlie, who was still at the table reading the newspaper; Spence could see his lips moving.

"Are you going tonight?" Sylvie asked, her smile turned on again.

Spence leaned forward and breathed in her perfume; she smelled like lilies. "Where?"

"Downtown. To watch the Frenchman. It's all Charlie's been talking about since he saw the story on the news."

"I don't know. You going?"

Her green eyes locked onto his. "No, I'll be home. Alone. Charlie's going down around five-thirty. You should come over."

Spence nodded, his body tingling at the thought of being with her again. She reached out and covered his hand with hers. He stared at the tanned fingers cupping his, marveling at their softness, remembering them touching other parts of his body on all those nights when Charlie was at the track or the casino or here at the OTB, gambling his disability check. He remembered their dexterity and the magic in them as she explored him, stroked him, loved him.

"Think about it," she said, and withdrew her hand.

As Spence walked back to the table, he knew that's all he'd be thinking about for the rest of the afternoon, that images of Sylvie—undressed, glistening, moving beneath him—would play in his mind like an illicit slideshow until he saw her that night and replaced those images with new ones of her, of them. All the vows he'd made to not see her again vanished.

Blind Charlie looked up, the overhead fluorescents reflecting off his glasses, so for a second it appeared there was nothing behind the lenses—no eyes, no pupils, no irises—just thick glass. "There's a thirty-percent chance of rain," he said.

Spence reached for his chair; he needed to sit down, his legs unsteady beneath him. He blinked several times at Charlie, trying to focus his thoughts. "At Monticello?" He tried to remember if Two Steppin' Tango was a mudder, but all he could think about was the way Sylvie's body felt and the sounds she made when she released.

"No. Here. He won't do the walk if it's raining. The wire has to be dry for at least an hour before he'll go on it. He wears leather dance shoes. The soles must get slick."

Spence looked at his hand, as if he could still feel Sylvie holding it. "You should go down early. Make sure you get a good spot."

Charlie nodded, paused, and then asked, "Who'd you bet on?"

"The five horse. Two Steppin' Tango."

"To win?"

"Show."

Charlie shook his head, a look of sadness washing over him. "You should have talked to me."

"She's a good horse."

"She's all over the place. You can't trust her."

Spence crossed and uncrossed his legs, then turned to the rows of televisions and watched the horses being led to the starting gate at Monticello. "It's a good wager."

"I'll bet she doesn't finish first, second, or third."

"Yeah? How much?"

"If she loses, you have to drive me down and help me find a spot to watch the Frenchman."

"And if she wins?"

"I'll match the payout. You'll double your winnings."

Spence reached across the table and shook Charlie's hand as the starting bell sounded from Monticello.

Two Steppin' Tango finished a nose out of the money. As Spence drove Blind Charlie down to find the best vantage point to watch the Frenchman fall, he wondered what excuse he could give to slip away and meet Sylvie once they found a good spot to watch the aerialist. Charlie sat in the passenger seat, his eyes closed, rambling on about what he had learned about Pasquette: how he had gone to circus school when he'd turned seventeen; how he'd started off with the Normandy Circus; how Philippe Petit, another Frenchman, had tutored him and made him his protégé.

"Who?" Spence asked, turning on Main Street.

"The guy who walked between the Twin Towers when there used to be Twin Towers," Charlie answered, his eyes still closed.

Charlie continued telling Pasquette's story and how he had learned a new word —funambulist—but Spence was no longer listening. He was thinking of Sylvie. She liked vintage clothes and would greet him at the door in nightgowns from the Thirties and Forties, sheer silk numbers that touched her ankles and had deep, scalloped necklines, or in lacey teddies, the peach, ivory, and mint fabrics contrasting with her tanned arms and thighs. He hoped she didn't greet Charlie in the same outfits, but he tried not to think of things like that too often.

Blind Charlie had stopped talking and was looking at Spence now, who realized that Charlie had asked him a question he hadn't heard. Spence covered up with a question of his own. "Why are you so interested in the high wire anyway?"

Charlie looked at him like Spence was the one who couldn't see. "It's the ultimate gamble, Spence. The stakes don't get any higher. When guys like you and me lose, we hock our watches or sell our furniture. But when an aerialist loses, it's all over. Can you imagine risking it all, Spence? Can you imagine a pot that big?"

"Must be a hell of a feeling if you win."

"Yeah, but if you lose…"

Spence parked near the Liberty Building, and they stood on the sidewalk looking up, their heads tilted back, like tourists who had never seen a tall building before.

"I need to be higher," Charlie said. Binoculars hung around his neck, the ones he took to the track. "And facing north or south so I can see the whole length of the wire."

"He's going to be pretty high up, Charlie. He'll look tiny. Are you sure you'll be able to see him at all?"

Charlie set his jaw. "I'll see him. I just have to get higher."

Spence looked around at the surrounding buildings. The Rand Building was the right height but didn't offer a clear view of the wire. The Central Library wasn't high enough, not by a long shot. City Hall's Observation Deck was actually three or four stories above the Liberty Building but faced the wrong way.

"There," Spence said, pointing south to a black and glass office building. "Main Place Tower. That should be perfect."

Blind Charlie smiled.

The Liberty Building and Main Place Tower, a twenty-six story office building filled with law and architectural firms, insurance companies, and advertising agencies, were connected by a dying shopping mall. Spence and Blind Charlie walked to the entrance and then cut through the deserted mall, passing darkened stores, their entrances gated and padlocked. Faded signs, *Available* and *Vacancy*, hung forgotten from the gating. Some signs had come loose and fallen and were covered by dusty footprints. The stores that remained open—discount shoe stores, dollar stores, T-shirt places—had few customers, and the ones who were there picked at the merchandise as if they had nothing better to do, lifting items off the shelves and racks and returning them without even glancing at the price tags. No one noticed Spence and Charlie or stopped them as they made their way to the Tower's elevators at the south end of the mall, the pair moving like they had purpose and belonged. The security desk was unattended, and they hurried by, afraid someone would appear and yell at them to stop. When the elevator doors shut and Charlie pressed the button for the top floor, they turned to each other and smiled as they shot skyward, like they had gotten away with something.

The stairwell was near the elevator, and when they got off at the twenty-sixth floor, they hurried up to the roof, taking the steps two at a time, their shoes echoing off the metal. Spence could already feel Sylvie's pull, as if the closer he got to the roof, the stronger her draw was on him from the other side of town, like gravity tugging at him. Sylvie knew she had this power over him; it was nearly impossible for Spence to leave her bed, and Sylvie delighted in this, keeping him there as long as possible with soft whispers and her softer body pressed against his. Spence would struggle to leave, both of them knowing that it was getting late, that Charlie could be back any moment. Once she called him on his way home, her voice breathless and excited, telling him that Charlie had missed him by three minutes.

"What if the door's locked?" Charlie asked, breathing hard from the climb.

"I think they have to keep it open. Fire codes or something," Spence answered, but he was already thinking of another door. He wondered what Sylvie would be wearing when she greeted him. He hoped for garters and stockings.

The door leading to the roof opened with a push. Charlie had been right; it was windy that high up. The breeze off the lake tousled their hair and Spence could smell Cheerios wafting from the General Mills plant on the waterfront, the grain elevators clearly visible.

"Jesus, we're high," Spence said. "I can see Canada."

The entire city spread before him, and he was surprised at how close everything was to each other—the lake, the new windmills where Bethlehem Steel once stood, the arena. It was as if his world had suddenly grown smaller as soon as he stepped onto the roof.

"Look," Charlie said, walking to the north end of the building with his arm raised, pointing and moving to the very edge. The cuffs of his pants fluttered in the wind.

Pasquette's wire, a dark line bisecting the blue sky, was attached to the statues at either end of the Liberty Building, waiting for him; any chance of rain, of delaying the walk, had burned away with the September sun. Spence followed and stood at the precipice beside Charlie, who pressed the binoculars against his thick lenses.

"I can see perfectly," Charlie said.

From below, Spence heard an ambulance's siren and cars honking. He wondered if Pasquette would hear traffic noises, too, or if he'd be concentrating so intently on the next step that he'd be oblivious to all traffic sounds and the cheers pouring out from people watching from rooftops and office windows. He wondered if he'd be able to hear Charlie yelling for him to fall.

"Can you imagine *walking* on that?" Spence asked. "How the hell does he do it?"

"He uses a pole for balance," Charlie answered. He took a few steps back, his binoculars still raised. "But that first step on the wire must be the scariest of them all, don't you think?"

"I think it's all scary," Spence answered, looking over the edge and down to the sidewalk below, his eyes tearing from the wind. Vertigo gripped him. Only Sylvie and the chance at stealing a few hours with her could have gotten him on this windy rooftop, he thought. He wondered if she were thinking of him and counting the minutes until he arrived.

"But the first step must be the worst," Charlie continued. "He knows at that moment that it's wrong for him to be there, that it's not natural. He can stop then, call it all off, but he doesn't. Then he takes another step and another. Until there's no turning back. He's gone too far. He's got to go through with it now and see it to the very end, no matter what. He's got to risk it all, man. Let it ride. There's nothing and no one to save him now."

"One mistake and you're fucked," Spence said, looking at the wire, trying to picture the Frenchman in his hand-painted costume and leather dance shoes making his way from one end of the line to the other, lifting his foot and then setting it down precisely, over and over, until the end, just as he had done in Paris, London, Copenhagen, and all those other towns and cities where he'd gambled it all and won.

"That's right, Spence," Charlie said. "That's exactly right."

Spence wondered if anyone would wait for the Frenchman—a wife, a girl friend, a lover—at the other end of the wire, her breath held, her hands clasped, a prayer on her soft lips colored his favorite shade. Spence hoped so, imagining Pasquette's eyes never leaving her as he made his way across the sky to where she waited as if he were crossing that lonely emptiness just so he could step off that wire and into her arms where it was safe and there was no chance of falling. He pictured Sylvie waiting there, the Lake Erie wind blowing back her highlighted hair and melding the vintage nightgown to her body, the silk clinging to every curve, her arms outstretched, open, empty.

Before Spence could ask if the Frenchman was married, he felt Charlie's breath on his neck and heard him whisper Sylvie's name in his ear before he felt the hard shove between his shoulder blades. Then he was over the side, off the wire, his arms flailing like a bird desperate to take flight, slipping through the wind somewhere between heaven and earth, with no safety net or harness to save him.

Games

Originally published in *Verb*

sat holding the money, watching Cool Louie go one-on-one with a black kid named Ray-Ray. We didn't belong on Peach Street, but C.L. said not to worry because he had it covered, and I wondered what he meant by that. He usually only played against local talent at the park, but he needed money. His sister, Anna, had developed a habit and paid for it by hustling. When Louie found out, he decided to buy the shit for her to get her off her back. I had to turn my head when he asked me for money.

Anna already had my cash.

Ray-Ray was playing near the rim, slapping back all of C.L.'s shots. His purple-black skin gleamed with sweat as he glided by dribbling the ball; the sound of rubber bouncing against asphalt echoed across the playground like it did every summer day from dawn till dark. Ray-Ray wore sweatpants cut at the knees and three wristbands to his elbow; his every move seemed effortless. A hand would snake out, knocking the ball away, or he'd spin past Louie and seem suspended in air before slamming it through. He ran the score five-zip, and all the brothers who lined the fence, their fingers laced through the diamond openings, waited for their shot at the money. They cheered for Ray-Ray each time the ball dropped through the rim.

C.L. called time to tie his high-tops and catch his breath. He took a towel from his gym bag under the basket and wiped his face.

I held the two twenties in my fist. A couple days earlier, C.L. had played against Frankie Aronica at the park. Jimmy J. was holding the bets, but he got careless and started watching the game too closely. A

Puerto Rican kid ran by, knocked him down, and took off with the cash. He was over the fence and gone before anyone could move. C.L. took it out on Jimmy. He beat him bad, busting up his face and yelling that the money was for Anna.

Jimmy J. doesn't hang out at the park anymore. We're still looking for the Puerto Rican kid.

C.L. backed his way toward the hoop, keeping his body between Ray-Ray and the ball. At about eight feet he spun and with a flick of the wrist shot a beautiful fade-away jumper. The ball arched towards the basket and scraped through the chain net.

Ray-Ray shook his shaved head, and the kid next to me turned up the music. C.L. took the ball out again, but Ray-Ray didn't even guard him, challenging him to hit another J because the first was just luck. C.L. nailed it.

A black-and-white cruised by, making sure no one was dealing on the playground. I saw the crook of the cop's elbow resting on the door and heard the static from the police radio. Green glass from broken bottles crunched under the tires. Peach Street was even worse than our neighborhood. My mom wants to send me out of the projects to live with my aunt. She says the proj is no place for a kid to grow up and nothing good will come of me here.

I don't want to move.

I'd miss the park: Cool Louie raining jumpers, Anna putting out on picnic tables, us shaking down the fags in the shadows for a couple of bucks and some laughs.

The score was tied at six when it turned ugly. Ray-Ray was driving hard when C.L. stuck his knee out, tripping him. The brothers behind me started yelling. Ray-Ray didn't say anything, but the next time he boxed out, an elbow caught C.L. in the throat.

The play seemed to progress in slow motion after that. Ray-Ray grabbed the rebound and hung in the air. C.L. cut his legs out from under him. He landed on all fours, leaving his palms and knees scraped raw.

I could feel the fence shaking.

The ball bounced to the spray-painted foul line, and C.L. chased it down. Ray-Ray got up and let him drive the lane. As C.L. leaped for the layup, Ray-Ray pushed him hard from behind, carrying him into the green pole that held the backboard. C.L. bounced off the pole and landed on his back, but Ray-Ray pulled him up by the hair and rammed a knee into his face. I squeezed the bills tight, feeling my pulse in my fingertips.

Ray-Ray would be coming for the money now.

Blood streamed from Cool Louie's nostrils and his upper lip was split wide. His eyes looked unfocused, the way they did when he told me about Anna.

As Ray-Ray turned to face me, C.L. reached in his gym bag. He brought out the blade and the games ended with a flick of the wrist.

Stealing Ted Williams' Head

Originally published in *Hayden's Ferry Review*

O'Brien and I were watching a documentary on ESPN, grainy, black and white footage of baseball's greatest sluggers, when he decided that we should steal Ted Williams' head. The lights in the living room were turned off and the volume on the television kept low, so I could barely hear Lowell Thomas, the Movietone news announcer, report that Williams had ended the 1941 season with a .406 batting average, the last Major Leaguer to hit over .400. We were trying to keep the noise down. My daughter, Elena, a newborn, was asleep, swaddled in my arms, smelling of diaper cream and lotion, and my wife, Annie, was upstairs in bed, resting until the next feeding.

"What would we do with it?" I asked.

Ted Williams was on the screen again, this time in a suit, not a Red Sox uniform, being inducted into the Marine Corp just seven months after hitting .406, his head clearly and securely attached, his body whole.

O'Brien stared at me, his arm raised, a beer suspended in air, inches short of his mouth. "We'd bury it, stupid. In Fenway. In left field where he played." He put the bottle to his mouth, tilted his head, and drained it like I'd seen him do a thousand times over the years. Maybe ten thousand.

I shook my head and shifted my daughter to my other arm. She weighed nothing, everything. Six pounds, eight ounces at birth. "You're crazy, O'Brien. Or drunk."

We were more than a decade removed from high school, creeping closer to our thirties with our hairlines receding and our waistlines expanding, but we still called each other only by our last names, just as we had as adolescents. Our other buddies from high school—Ferg, Naylon, Fehan—had all left Buffalo years ago for better jobs and warmer temperatures. O'Brien was the last tie to my childhood.

"Why can't we?" he asked, his face slack from beer and partially illuminated by the flickering television. He reached for the last bottle in the twelve-pack by his feet and opened it. "He'd want us to."

I started to argue that neither Ted Williams nor his severed head knew us from Adam, so how the hell could he want us to steal anything? But O'Brien hushed me and used the remote to turn up the television's volume. Elena stirred at the increased sound and scrunched her face. Her lips, delicate and perfect like her mother's, worked in her sleep, dreaming, perhaps, of nursing. I rocked her until she settled.

"This is it," O'Brien said, and we both watched as the documentary described Williams' death and what happened afterwards.

Williams—"The Splendid Splinter", "The Thumper", "Teddy Ballgame", "The Kid"—was 83 when he died of cardiac arrest. His will instructed that his remains be cremated and spread over the Florida Keys, a place that he'd loved and fished since retiring from baseball. However, his son, John Henry, claimed that Williams had changed his mind and wanted his body frozen and his brain, containing all that baseball and hitting knowledge, preserved until science and tissue regeneration technology evolved to a point where a new body could be regrown. John Henry produced a handwritten note signed by his father and dated after the will was filed stating this. He had the corpse sent to a cryonics lab in Arizona where Ted Williams' vitrified head was surgically removed, placed in a steel can, and immersed in liquid nitrogen. His sister objected, arguing that John Henry was preserving the body not for a future resurrection, but so he could sell their father's DNA.

"I believe the sister," O'Brien said, setting his beer down hard for emphasis. It foamed all over the coffee table, a piece inherited from Annie's grandmother. I tossed him a spit-up cloth to blot it.

"Eight DNA samples are missing," he said, wiping the spilled beer. "What happened to them?"

Elena began to fuss in her sleep; she'd be awake soon, her little mouth an oval as she wailed for food. "I don't know, O'Brien. Turn the volume down."

"We got to steal it, Weber. It's the right thing to do."

A picture of the Alcor Life Extension Foundation in Scottsdale, Arizona filled the screen, the facility storing Ted Williams' head. The windowless building, low and gray, looked like a modern warehouse rather than a medical or science facility. Palm trees grew on either end of the building, framing the picture like a postcard.

O'Brien stood, wavering a bit, still dressed from work in a dirty Red Sox cap, camouflage shorts, and grass-stained boots; he smelled like sunscreen and bug spray. He had started his landscaping business in tenth grade, mowing the widows' lawns on our street, and had grown his customer list over the years so he was now cutting grass and trimming hedges eight hours a day, six days a week. In the winter, he hooked a plow to the front of his truck and cleared snow from driveways and parking lots, an upgrade from when we were kids and shoveled everything by hand for movie money.

He pointed toward the television. "That's where we're going, bud. You and me. Just like old times. Bust in, grab Teddy, and bury him in Fenway."

"How? There's no windows. They probably have alarms and cameras and guard dogs."

O'Brien headed to the front door, staggering slightly, and swatted away my objections with a wave of his arm. "Leave it to me." He slammed the door behind him, startling Elena awake. She began to howl.

I didn't hear from O'Brien for a while after that. This wasn't unusual; weeks or months would sometimes pass without a word from him, and then he'd show up at my door, his arms filled with beer and Cheetos like we were still teenagers. But we were no longer in high school and circled in different orbits now. My life revolved around work, then rushing home to help Annie with the baby—rocking and walking her when she was cranky, bathing her, and then the feedings every three hours. O'Brien's life, a life I envied when Elena refused to sleep, centered on cutting lawns, playing softball twice a week, and chasing pretty Latina girls at Voelkers Bowling Alley.

The idea of stealing Ted Williams' head was soon forgotten and filed away with all the other schemes O'Brien had come up with over the years: taking the signed Springsteen poster, circa 1975, that was framed and bolted to the wall at Voelkers, the one with the black Chuck Taylors dangling off the end of his Telecaster; cutting down pine trees at Delaware Park and selling them on the corner as fresh Christmas trees that December when we were both dead broke; buying the Stumble Inn, our old hangout after high school, that stood vacant and boarded up for years. In each case, O'Brien would become excited about the idea when it first hit him and would start making elaborate plans, scribbling notes and diagrams on cocktail napkins, but the next day the great ideas melted away in sobriety's hot light. We never stole the poster, cut the trees, or bought the bar.

Then, around late August, when the nights were growing cooler and the pennant races were heating up, O'Brien began sending texts and leaving messages. He left the first message at the office. I worked as a technical writer but never considered what I did for a living as writing. I was a counter of spaces, an indentation specialist, a master of the simple sentence. I produced manuals on how to use my company's inventory-control software, but it wasn't writing. It was formatting, making sure there were four blank lines, not three or five, following a screen shot and that commands, like F12, were boldface and not italicized. Each day I settled behind my desk like I was settling into the dentist's chair.

He had left the message sometime during the night, so my phone was flashing in my gray cube that morning. I wasn't sure why he hadn't called me at home. Maybe it was too late and he didn't want to wake

Annie or Elena. Most likely he just dialed the office number by mistake. He didn't say hello or even identify himself in the message, but I recognized O'Brien's voice, even though it was thick and slurred. In the background I heard music and ricocheting bowling pins. The message was brief; he said that it was 2,200 miles from Buffalo to Scottsdale and we could make it in thirty-six hours if we took turns driving and his truck didn't break down. He hung up without saying goodbye. Later that day, while in a meeting regarding pagination, I received a text: *2,683 miles from Scottsdale to Fenway. I have shovels.*

I pictured us in O'Brien's dented pickup, driving with the windows open, the wind blowing back our thinning hair, and the music so loud I could feel the bass thumping in my chest. A cooler filled with beer and sandwiches sat between us; a half-smoked blunt waited for us in the ashtray. We'd talk about the Tripi sisters, Paula and Franny, and argue which one was hotter, just like we had since Little League. We'd stop at roadside attractions along the way—the water tower in Licking, Missouri painted like a baseball; the world's largest pop bottle off of Route 66; James Dean's grave in Indiana—and have our pictures taken at all of them. As we rolled through the night with just the stars and our high beams lighting the way, I'd tune in ballgames on the AM dial and we'd listen to the staticy play-by-play calls, even if they were just minor league games broadcasted from Midwestern towns we'd never heard of. When we drove out of range, I'd turn the dial again until I found another game played by teams with names like the Mud Hens, the Lumber Kings, and the Doubledays.

Imagining the trip, making up conversations, and picturing the places we'd drive by somehow got me through to five o'clock when I could escape my cube and go home.

That night, Annie greeted me at the door. Her hair was pulled back in a ponytail; dark circles raccooned her eyes and she wore no make-up. She said she was going to an exercise class with her sister or maybe to the mall. It didn't matter; she just needed to get out of the house for a while. Bottles of expressed breast milk were in the refrigerator and new nipples were boiling on the stove, becoming sterilized at that very moment. There was leftover pizza for me.

"Oh," she said, grabbing her purse. "O'Brien called. He sounded weird."

"O'Brien always sounds weird," I said.

"I didn't understand the message. He said 'Thumper's head is in can A-1949'. Who's Thumper?"

"Ted Williams."

"The baseball player?"

I nodded. "O'Brien wants to steal his head."

Elena began to cry from the next room, her nap over. Annie glanced toward the cries and hurried toward the door. "I won't be late," she said, without giving Ted Williams, his head, or me a second thought.

I went to Elena, scooped her in my arms, and kissed her cheeks and forehead. Why A-1949? I wondered, as I walked into the kitchen. After Elena was fed, changed and gurgling in my arms, I looked up Ted Williams' stats on the Internet. In 1949, he hit 43 homeruns, the most he'd ever hit in a single season. I wondered if that had anything to do with the numbering scheme, if the folks at the Alcor Life Extension Foundation were morbid baseball fans and knew Teddy Ballgame's statistics, or if his can number was merely randomly assigned from a crappy inventory-control system like mine and could easily have been used to track a milk carton or olive jar instead of baseball's greatest hitter's head.

Then Elena, who was just dozing off, snapped awake in my arms, her eyes wide as if startled, and began to shriek. Her face turned red and her tiny fists clenched as she howled. I put her on my shoulder, rubbed her back, and tried to burp her, certain she was suffering from gas. I patted gently from her lower back up to her shoulder blades and down again, cooing softly in her ear the whole time, but she only cried harder. Her diaper was clean and dry, but the crying jag continued. She slapped away another warmed bottle of breast milk when I put the nipple to her mouth.

Her wailing scared me. She had never cried with such intensity before. Her face pinched together in agony, and she sounded as if she were in pain. Words, whose exact medical definitions were unclear to me, starting flashing in my mind—encephalitis, meningitis, and a few other conditions ending in itis that I think I made up. The leftover pizza, eaten quickly and unheated, felt leaden in my stomach.

Each time I called, Annie's cell phone went to voicemail.

The more Elena cried the more rattled I became. I pleaded with her to stop, promising her puppies and ponies and a convertible if she'd just go to sleep. I called my mother in Florida, who said she sounded colicky and that I should try walking and singing to her. We paced the length of the living room so many times that I was certain I was wearing a groove in the hardwood floor and leaving a trail of sawdust in my wake. I sang seventy-two choruses of "Wheels on the Bus" that night, ending with:

> *The father on the bus jumped out the window,*
> *Jumped out the window,*
> *Jumped out the window.*

Elena screamed even louder when I set her carrier on the running dryer, hoping the noise and vibration would put her to sleep. Her puffed cheeks turned crimson and she shrieked until snot and saliva mixed together. I rescued her from her carrier and bounced her in my arms while I shifted my weight from one foot to the other, telling her to "look at Daddy dance. Look at Daddy dance." Her crying paused and she studied me with her mother's eyes, finally deciding I was moronic, something she's not supposed to do until she's a teenager, and began wailing louder.

Three hours later, when she'd finally stopped crying, when she'd exhausted herself to sleep, I slipped her into her crib, being careful not to wake her, then collapsed in the Lazyboy, my head pounding and my nerves jangled. I felt drained and like crying myself when O'Brien sent me another text: *The can is as big as a lobster pot.*

For the next week, starting around 5:30 when I got home, Elena would cry for hours. Nothing we tried consoled her; our pediatrician told us she was fine, that some babies do this, to let her cry. Our house, a starter home, was small, a little under fifteen hundred square feet, and Elena's shrieks bounced off each thin wall and filled every corner, boring their way into our skulls and patience. Annie and I would sit at the table, our dinners untouched, feeling tortured and helpless as the crying went on and on and on. I'd try to distract Annie by telling her about some major font controversy at work or how O'Brien wanted to steal Ted Williams' head, but at some point Annie would start crying, covering her face with her hands or weeping into her napkin. Between sobs she'd whisper that we were failed parents.

When O'Brien called one night and told me that he had worked out a plan to steal Ted Williams' head and to meet him at Voelkers, I grabbed my keys and headed for the door. I moved fast, like I was rounding second, so Annie couldn't stop me.

I hadn't been in Voelkers in years, not since I was single and they'd sponsored our softball team. We'd come in after the games and drink pitchers of Canadian beer and eat chicken wings until they kicked us out at 4 a.m. While my life had changed completely since those days, nothing had changed at Voelkers. The green neon letters still flashed "BOWLING" near the roof, and a smaller neon sign above the side door still showed an orange ball moving toward white pins until it struck them. Smoking in public places had been banned for ten years, but Voelkers still smelled of cigarettes when I walked in; ashtrays sat defiantly on the oval bar. Out of habit, I turned to the right where the Springsteen poster had always hung, but it was gone, the plaster cracked where someone had ripped the bolts from the wall.

The bar was empty. It was too early for the bowling leagues' evening matches, and the softball teams hadn't come in yet. O'Brien was nowhere in sight. I took a seat on my old stool, the one facing the door, the spot I had always tried to claim so I'd be the first to see the girls when they walked in. I ordered a beer from the pretty bartender with permed dark hair. She was a good ten years younger than me, wearing tight jeans and a tighter tank top with Voelkers stretched across her rounded breasts. She set the sweating bottle in front of me without giving me a glance, her attention fixed on Alex Trebek and *Jeopardy* on the flat screen. The lanes behind me were quiet.

"Hey," O'Brien said, sliding onto the stool next to me, a manila folder in his hand. He had come in the side door, under the neon ball and pins, a strike thrown every time.

"Hey," I answered.

I looked at our reflections in the mirror behind the bar. O'Brien's face was lean and tanned from working in the sun and playing softball. My skin had the gray look of someone who spent his days in a windowless cube and his nights walking an inconsolable child. His birthday was three months before mine, but I looked years older.

The bartender brought him a beer without waiting for him to order.

"The poster's gone," I said, peeling the label off my bottle without tearing it, a sign of good luck.

O'Brien glanced toward the empty space where the Springsteen poster had hung, the rectangle of paint clean and bright compared to the rest of the wall. "Somebody swiped it last weekend. There was a fight back by the pool tables. They grabbed it during all the commotion when no one was looking."

"Was it you?"

His face sagged, as if his eyebrows and tanned cheeks were suddenly too heavy and couldn't be supported by his bones and tendons. He shook his head. "No, some kid must have gotten it," he said, his voice sounding as old and tired as I felt.

"We should have stolen it years ago."

"We should have done a lot of things."

We clinked bottles. A quiet sadness settled on us like lightly falling snow, as if both of us were remembering the turns we had taken and the ones we had missed to get to this point in our lives. I would have given anything then for a pack of kids to burst through the door, waving their college IDs so they could get free shoe rental, hoping their laughter and unwavering belief that everything would turn out all right in their lives would rub off on us. No one came in, so I asked O'Brien what was in the manila folder.

He sat straighter on his barstool and opened it, his body suddenly alive. The first thing he pulled out was an old Texaco roadmap. We moved our beer bottles aside so he could spread it open. With a finger still dirty from landscaping, he traced the highlighted route to Scottsdale: the New York State Thruway all the way to Pennsylvania, across Ohio and Indiana, then four hundred miles on 44 West, another eight hundred miles on Highway 40, finally winding through Arizona state roads until we got to Scottsdale.

I pictured us again in O'Brien's truck, rolling across America with the windows down and the radio tuned to a ballgame, a good two thousand miles away from how our lives had turned out, increasing the distance with each rotation of the tires.

O'Brien shoved the map aside without bothering to fold it, his voice excited now, rushing his words together. He pulled turn-by-turn directions to 7895 East Acoma Drive from the folder—the address of the Alcor Life Extension Foundation, the home of Ted Williams' head—and read off the street names like they were holy: East Shea, North Hayden, East Acoma.

"Everything's on the internet, Weber. Everything," he said, handing me the photos he had printed.

I flipped through images of the facility taken from all angles, even a series shot from a satellite, as if we were planning a coordinated air strike to spring Teddy's head.

"And they only have ten employees," O'Brien went on. "There's no night shift, Weber. None."

"What about guards?" I asked, handing back the photographs. "And there's still no windows except those big front ones and we can't break those."

"Who guards frozen dead people? And *we're* not going to break in. *I'm* going to break *out*. We're going to pretend we're landscaping, pruning those desert bushes there," he said, pointing to a photograph with that dirty finger again. "Or raking those stones they got out front. Then I'll sneak in and hide somewhere. You'll drive off in the truck like we've finished working and park nearby. At five o'clock when everyone leaves, I'll start looking for can A-1949. It shouldn't take long. There's only eighty bodies frozen in there and some of those are animals. You know, pets. Cats and dogs that rich people hope they can thaw out one day. I'll find Ted Williams' head in no time."

"I don't get to go in?"

A man entered the bowling alley and sat at the bar across from us. O'Brien lowered his voice. "You'll be my eyes outside, my man. We'll have radios and you'll tell me when the parking lot's empty. That's when I'll start looking for Teddy Ballgame. When I find him, I'll call you on the walkie-talkie to bring the truck around and then we're off to Fenway."

The man across the bar from me was my age, maybe a little older. He wore a rumpled blue suit, his skin as cube-gray as mine, and was trying to tell the pretty bartender a joke about two naked nuns hanging wall paper, but she was more interested in the Final Jeopardy! question. He wouldn't give up though, starting the joke over a couple times, hoping to get her attention and make her smile, oblivious to the fact that she wasn't interested and never would be. The man's gray face started looking more like my own, and I wanted to yell at him to shut the fuck up, to stop being pathetic, that he didn't have a shot with someone that young and pretty. He started the joke a third time.

"When do we leave?" I asked, trying to ignore the man in the suit.

"Five a.m. If you're not out after a couple minutes, I'll figure you're chicken shit and leave without you."

I glanced one more time at the man with the gray face, my gray face, and told O'Brien I'd be ready.

Lying next to Annie, I composed in my head the note I'd leave her, explaining what I was doing, where I was going, that I'd be home in a week. Sleep came in brief stretches—I'd snap awake, check the nightstand clock, wishing time would pass faster.

Annie woke while I was stuffing shorts in my duffle bag; it would be hot driving through the desert, and the air conditioning in O'Brien's truck hadn't worked since April. She flipped the lamp on, filling the room with murky light.

"What are you doing?" she mumbled, her voice dry sounding from sleep, her eyes squinting, not fully awake yet.

"I'm going with O'Brien to steal Ted Williams' head."

Her lips and eyebrows pinched together. "What?" Her face clouded. "What?"

"It's frozen. In Arizona. I told you about this."

She thought for a moment. I wasn't sure whether she was trying to remember our Ted Williams conversations or deciding if she was still dreaming. "Don't be stupid."

I shoved socks in my bag. O'Brien's truck rattled up outside our house, the brakes squeaking as he pulled to the curb.

Annie glanced at the window. "You're not leaving me alone with the baby."

"It's just a few days."

"I don't care how long it is, you're not going."

"I'll be home before you know it."

"You're not going."

I ignored her.

"What about work?"

"I have sick days coming. The indenting can wait."

"You'll get arrested, you know. Breaking and entering, trespassing, grave robbing."

O'Brien revved his engine, the sound calling me, and I wondered if his horn worked.

"It's not grave robbing."

"What do you call it then?" she asked, fully awake now, her voice like thrown knives.

"I don't know, but it's not *grave* robbing. There's no *grave* to rob. His head is frozen in a can."

"What happens when it thaws out?"

We hadn't considered that.

I stopped packing and wondered if we could drive to Boston and bury it before that happened, or, with no A/C, if we'd even make it out of the desert before Ted Williams' head started to melt. O'Brien pressed the gas again.

"Won't it smell?" she asked.

I zipped my duffle. "It'll be fine. I'll be fine."

Annie was sitting up now. "You're not going."

I showed her my duffle bag.

O'Brien's truck idled unevenly, like it could stall at any minute.

She cocked her head and smirked, a look that made me grip my bag tighter. "You and O'Brien never do anything. You talk about it. You make plans, but you never do anything. Then you talk about what you should've done. You two are still whining about things you didn't do *fifteen* years ago, for gods sake. I swear if I hear O'Brien say one more time how he should've asked out Paula Tripi I'll scream."

"This is different."

"How?"

"It just is," I said, and meant it. Stealing Ted Williams' head felt different, like we had to do this, like there was a finality to it, like if we didn't try, nothing would be possible again.

Annie folded her arms over her chest, her breasts full and heavy. She'd have to nurse soon. "I know you two. You'll get as far as Cleveland then turn around. You'll blame the truck or the weather, but you'll turn around all right."

I left our room without saying another word, my knuckles white as I clutched my bag. O'Brien tooted his horn twice—so it did work—and I hurried down the stairs. Two feet from the front door, Elena began to cry, the sound freezing me. This was her normal feeding-time cry, not the relentless wailing that haunted us in the evenings. I glanced at my watch; it was a little after five, time for her first meal. O'Brien revved his engine again. I waited to hear Annie's footsteps pad from our bedroom to the baby's room, the floorboards creaking in the hallway of our little house, but I heard nothing except O'Brien's truck and Elena's cries, which were increasing in volume as her hunger and frustration grew. At any minute I expected to hear Annie's soft voice calling to Elena, telling her it was okay, that mommy was coming, to hold on just one second, but Annie was silent. She couldn't have fallen back to sleep. Maybe she was in the bathroom.

I started up the stairs to get Elena, to hold and comfort her until Annie was ready for her. I considered warming a bottle, then stopped. An image of Annie flashed in front of me: she was propped on two pillows, the blankets covering her lap, her breasts exposed, waiting for me to bring Elena to her to nurse. She'd cock her head when I entered the bedroom carrying the baby, and she'd smirk, like she'd waited me out and won something.

I hurried down the stairs, my heart beating fast, determined to go through with O'Brien's crazy plan to steal Ted Williams' head, ignoring Elena, who was working herself up to an uncontrollable crying fit, an innocent caught in the middle of a power game of parental chicken. I unlocked the front door and turned the knob, gripped with the sense that I was finally doing something.

The morning air felt cool and was filled with the sounds of blue jays and cardinals, the grass wet with late summer dew. I hurried to the sidewalk, smelling O'Brien's exhaust, then froze and watched his truck head toward the corner, run the stop sign, then turn west, tires squealing. I stared at the corner a long time, as if his truck were still there, his brake lights still glowing red. Or maybe I thought he'd turn around and come back for me. I pictured him behind the wheel, a coffee cup or morning beer in his hand, gunning his truck towards the thruway and muttering Chicken shit, and I knew he wasn't coming back.

Swimming Naked

Originally published in *Young Adult Review Network*

stood outside the pool crouched forward, thin arms and skinny legs spread wide to cover as much wall as possible, my pubescent balls dangling like a target, waiting for the water polo game to begin. I don't know why we swam naked, but I suspect it was a way Mr. Jackson, our gym teacher with the *Smokey and the Bandit* mustache, could keep forty teenagers in line and submissive. There were no co-ed gym classes, and the girls didn't have to swim nude because of "female reasons", an excuse we boys found both unfair and unsatisfying. Instead, they received school-issued swimsuits color-coded by size: the petite girls swam in red suits, the average-built girls in black, and the heavy girls in an odd shade of blue that everyone called "Hippo Blue".

Mr. Jackson, dressed in sweatpants and a golf shirt, blew his whistle and tossed a rubber ball, the same red one we used in dodge ball, into the middle of the pool to start our version of a water polo match. The two teams, one in the deep end and one in the shallow, dove in and raced towards the ball to gain possession. Points were scored when the ball was thrown and hit the wall outside the pool below the painted black stripe, about waist-high, which was guarded by three naked, shivering goalies standing on the pool's deck. Sean McFarland, Ryan Connolly, and I had volunteered to guard our goal on that first water polo day. I wanted to play goalie because I was a poor swimmer and guessed that anyone with the ball would be forced underwater by a bunch of naked boys trying to wrestle it free, a thought that terrified me. Sean later said that he'd volunteered because the chlorine stung his eczema, the scaly pink patches that scarred his body and made him the object of ridicule in swim class; I think Ryan just wanted to keep his back to the wall, hiding the welts that crisscrossed his buttocks and back, the angry raised stripes left by his father's belt.

As I stood in my crouched position, determined to be the best damn water polo goalie because I was the worst damn swimmer in the entire school, I watched my classmates fight for the ball. It was impossible to tell which naked freshman was on my team and which was not. All I could see was splashed water, bare limbs and asses, and kids as small as Ryan and me getting shoved underwater by the early developers and the held-back kids, the hair under their arms and across their chests making them easy to spot.

The ball finally squirted free and Mark Jankowski grabbed it and began swimming toward me. No one tried to stop him; my teammates treaded water and let him pass. Jankowski was repeating the ninth grade for the second time and was the biggest kid in class, almost the same size as Mr. Jackson. Cradling the ball in one arm, he side-stroked his way to the shallow end of the pool until he was about five feet from me. He stood up, cocked his arm, and yelled as he threw the ball as hard as he could. The wet rubber smacked me in the shoulder, knocking me against the wall. The ball bounced back to Jankowski, who grabbed it and fired it at me again, this time catching me in the thigh and leaving a stinging red mark. Both teams cheered as I went down holding my leg.

After that, no one tried to throw the ball below the back stripe; they followed Jankowski's lead and aimed at the goalies instead, cheering loudest when the wet rubber ball left welts, smashed us in the genitals, or when we slipped on the slick deck and went sprawling, our tailbones and elbows striking the tiled floor, our heads banging against the wall if they were lucky.

I didn't try stopping the shots after Jankowski's first two throws. I tried to protect myself, punching the ball away or blocking it with my forearms, but even that was painful. Ryan and Sean didn't fare much better. One throw tore open an eczema scab on Sean's arm, and one of Jankowski's bullets smacked Ryan right in the gut.

"What hurts more, the ball or the belt?" Jankowski yelled to Ryan as he back-stroked away.

The ball finally made its way down to the other end of the pool. I squatted and hugged my knees for warmth, my thin shoulder and thigh still stinging from Jankowski's shots, and tried to make myself even smaller as I watched the other team's goalies become the naked targets. I was happy it was them getting bombarded and not me and hoped the ball stayed in their end for the rest of the match.

Afterward, I didn't say anything to Ryan or Sean as we showered our battered bodies, the bruises already forming; I was too embarrassed for them and myself to even make eye contact. But the next day, Ryan did something so extraordinary that it made me want to become his friend.

Swim class started normally. We had to shower before entering the pool. Mr. Tabor, the school janitor, stood in the doorway between the lockers and the shower room, and Mr. Jackson stood opposite of him in the doorway between the showers and the hallway leading to the pool, both watching us. They said they did this to keep an eye on us, to make sure there was no horseplay. Mr. Tabor grinned, as he always did, showing his dead front tooth, the faded tattooed anchors on his forearms visible, his hands buried in his pants pockets.

Then Ryan walked past Mr. Tabor into the showers wearing a pair of swim trunks. Conversations ended—the only sound was falling water. I turned to Mr. Jackson and saw his face darken, his Burt Reynolds mustache twitch.

"Connolly!" he boomed, his voice bouncing off the marble walls. "What are you wearing?"

"Swim trunks, coach," Ryan answered, soaping his chest like this was just another day.

"Why?" Mr. Jackson boomed again.

"Going swimming, coach," Ryan answered, his voice calm and even, cooler than I could ever be.

"Take them off!"

Ryan rinsed off the soap.

"You know the rules, Connolly. Get rid of them!"

Ryan started shampooing his hair.

"Are you going to take them off, Connolly?"

"Can't, coach. Swim class today."

The rest of us slunk out of the showers and toward the pool, not wanting to be caught in the middle of this. Mr. Jackson didn't even inspect us—making us turn for him, bend over, ensuring we'd rinsed all the soap from every part of our bodies before entering the pool; he just waived us to the metal bleachers. I glanced over my shoulder and saw Mr. Tabor's hands were out of his pockets and on his hips, his face as dark as Jackson's. Ryan was still under the shower.

I crossed my arms against my chest for warmth when I entered the pool area, the chlorine smell sharp in my nose. I sat on the cold metal bleachers, trying not to let my shoulders or legs touch the naked boy on either side of me as we waited. Everyone was quiet, even Jankowski and the other big kids who threw the water polo ball the hardest. I had my ear cocked, listening for Jackson to start screaming at Ryan, but heard nothing.

"What are they going to do to him?" Sean McFarland whispered.

"Nothing," Jankowski said. "They'll send him to the principal. Probably give him detention."

Jankowski's voice was deeper than the rest of ours and carried authority. He was always in trouble and walked the halls in black Levis and concert T-shirts—Zeppelin, Aerosmith, Rush—with the sleeves cut off. The taps on his square-toed boots clicked when he went by. He wore his hair parted in the middle and down to his shoulders like we all did, except his hair was thick and blonde as a Viking's. If anyone knew what Ryan's punishment would be, it would be Jankowski. So it surprised me a moment later when Ryan walked into the pool area still wearing his swim trunks. He took a seat on the bleachers with the rest of us. Mr. Jackson came in, still frowning, and started calling attendance, spitting our names through his teeth and checking us off on his clipboard with an angry wrist flick.

When he was done taking roll, Jackson smoothed his mustache with his index finger and slapped the clipboard against his leg. I jumped at the sound, remembering the time he had smacked it across my bare ass for running near the water's edge.

"As you can see," he said, "Mr. Connolly has decided to bring in trunks today. I told him this wasn't necessary. I could've borrowed a red suit from the girls for him to wear."

Jankowski laughed the loudest.

"Mr. Connolly declined this offer and he also declined to take off his trunks and swim naked like the rest of you men," he said, even though Jankowski was the only one of us anywhere near manhood. "So, we're going to sit here until Mr. Connolly takes off his suit and follows the rules."

Everyone groaned, including me. The only way to stay warm during swim class was to get in the water. To sit naked and wet on metal bleachers for forty minutes would be torture and we all knew it.

"Asshole," Jankowski muttered, not to Mr. Jackson but to Ryan.

In ten minutes, my skin puckered in goose bumps. In fifteen, my teeth chattered. It felt as if the metal bleachers were sucking the heat from inside me, drawing it from my marrow and out my legs and ass and scrotum as I squirmed trying to stay warm.

"Just take them off, Ryan," somebody whispered.

"This sucks," someone else said.

"Take them off," Jankowski said, "or I'll beat your ass like your old man does."

Ryan rubbed his arms for warmth but didn't make a move to take off his trunks.

More and more kids began whispering for him to come on, to take them off, that they were freezing, for chrissakes. A Joe's Boy, a new kid who had transferred from St. Joe's after getting expelled, sat a row higher than Ryan and kicked him in the kidneys and whispered *Come on* whenever Mr. Jackson wasn't looking.

I didn't say anything. My hands and head shook, but I wanted him to keep his trunks on, thinking that somehow his stand would make Mr. Jackson give in and we could all wear bathing suits. But Mr. Jackson didn't budge and neither did Ryan. We spent the entire forty minutes freezing on the bleachers. I couldn't remember ever feeling so cold.

"That's the class, gentleman," Jackson said, when the bell rang. "We'll sit here like this tomorrow if Mr. Connolly decides to break the rules again."

"Wear 'em tomorrow and you're dead," Jankowski said to Ryan loud enough for Mr. Jackson to hear. Jackson said nothing. He just slapped the clipboard against his leg.

As each boy hurried past Ryan to get to the warm showers, they made sure to bump him with their shoulder, jab an elbow to his ribs, or whisper a threat if he wore the trunks again. I patted his back when I walked by. He hurried and dressed and got the hell out of the locker room before Jankowski and the rest of them finished showering.

News of Ryan and his swim trunks spread through school. When I told the story, my friends' eyes saucered in amazement until I got to the part about sitting on the bleachers. Then they shook their heads, muttered what a jerk he was, and said they were glad they weren't in that class. Ryan's hall locker was about seven away from mine. Kids walked by, pointed, some shoved him.

After school, I was at my locker grabbing my jacket when I looked up and saw Ryan hurrying away. I didn't blame him. Fast-deserting hallways were a bad place to be when you were a target. The new kid from St. Joe's flipped the books out of Ryan's hand as he rushed by, and notes scattered across the floor. Other kids heading for the exit stepped on them. Someone kicked his history book all the way to the drinking fountain.

"Don't wear your bikini tomorrow, asshole," the Joe's Boy called over his shoulder as he walked away. Some sophomore girls laughed.

I helped Ryan gather his papers and tried to straighten them and brush away the dusty footprints, the treads and sneaker soles clearly visible across the pages. Ryan's face was blank, unreadable. If he was mad or scared, he didn't show it. Only his lips, pressed together in a hard line, revealed anything.

"Wearing the trunks took some guts, man," I said, and picked up his science notes. Delicate sketches he had made of the leaves we were studying covered the pages—petiolated, sessile, lobed—and rosebuds, shaded red in colored pencil.

"Thanks," he mumbled, trying to shove the papers back through the binder rings.

"Swimming naked is fucked up." I handed him his notes.

Ryan looked at me, his eyes flat, gray. "Then wear yours tomorrow."

"What?"

"If you think it's fucked up, which it is, wear your suit. If a bunch of us wear them, what are they going to do? Send us all down to the office? Big deal. Getting yelled at or detention is still better than swimming naked or getting killed in water polo."

Now it was my turn for my eyes to saucer. "You're going to wear them *again*?"

Ryan nodded. "And so will you if you have any balls." He turned and headed to the drinking fountain to retrieve his history book, a jumble of notes under his arm. I stood there, my body electric with the idea of taking a stand.

For the rest of the day, my mind kept drifting back to the idea of wearing swim trunks to class. I imagined strutting past Tabor like he and his hungry eyes didn't exist. Different comebacks, each one cooler than the previous one, came to me when I thought of Mr. Jackson asking me what the hell I was doing. I pictured the other kids, after seeing me and Ryan in our trunks, pulling their own from their lockers and putting them on, so only Jankowski and the other assholes were standing naked with their dicks hanging out. Their stunned expressions floated before me like plates to be smashed with a baseball bat.

The next morning I hesitated before packing my trunks in my book bag, pushing them to the bottom, covering them with notebooks and folders.

I saw Ryan before homeroom, but I didn't tell him about the swim trunks in my book bag. His black eye and swollen lip made me turn away. As I worked my hall locker combination, my fingers trembling a bit, I wondered who'd beaten him, Jankowski or the Joe's Boy.

Or both.

I wondered how badly they'd beat me if I wore my trunks that afternoon.

Then I stopped turning the dial and stared at my closed locker. Maybe it wasn't anybody from school who had blackened his eye. Maybe Mr. Jackson had called Ryan's parents and told them what a troublemaker their son was and his father had decided to use his fist instead of his belt this time.

My head snapped around when I heard the unmistakable sound of a body being slammed against metal. The hall went quiet. Jankowski had Ryan jacked up against the lockers, a fistful of shirt in his hand. He was shouting in Ryan's face not to wear his trunks today, that he wasn't going to freeze his ass off again. Ryan turned his head. I'm not sure how big Ryan's dad was, but he must have been bigger than Jankowski because there was no fear in Ryan's eyes, just resignation.

I was half the size of Jankowski, but if I came from behind, grabbed his shoulder and spun him, I knew I could get a punch off, one good shot to his nose or mouth. It wouldn't be enough. He wouldn't hold his hands to his bleeding lips and run away; he'd come for me, and I wouldn't be able to stop him. Neither Ryan nor I were strong enough to beat a guy like Jankowski, but together I knew we could take him. Ryan, I swear, nodded at me, as if he were reading my mind, urging me to do it, to spin Jankowski's shoulder, to throw that one good punch. Then I saw Ryan's black eye and the way Jankowski's arm bulged in his cutoff Stones shirt, and I didn't move. A long moment passed and Ryan nodded again, as if accustomed to no one rescuing him. Jankowski kneed him in the balls before letting go of his collar. Ryan crumpled to the floor. The warning bell rang and I headed to homeroom, feeling smaller than I ever had.

For the rest of the morning, I avoided going to my locker between classes, afraid I'd run into Ryan, afraid he'd call me a coward, just afraid in general. In each class, I'd pull out a binder or textbook, being careful to keep the trunks covered so no one could see them, point to them, tell Jankowski about them. I regretted bringing them and my regret added to my shame.

I made it to lunch without running into Ryan again. There was a seat open at the table where Sean McFarland sat, so I slid across from him, my tray piled with pizza slices, mashed potatoes, and chocolate pudding with perfect whipped cream dollops. Gorging myself was my latest attempt at gaining weight, at getting bigger.

"You going to eat all that?" Sean asked, nodding to my tray. As usual, he wore a long-sleeved turtleneck, trying to keep any eczema on his arms and neck covered, saving the ridicule for swim class.

Before I could answer, everyone in the cafeteria rose and cheered like at a football game. A fight had broken out. A tight circle of students formed to keep the teachers and cafeteria monitors from breaking up the brawl too quickly. Sean and I jumped to our feet and pushed to the ring of students. In the center of the circle, Ryan and Jankowski fought.

Each held the other's shirt with their left hand and traded wild right hand punches to the other's head. The crowd cheered as each blow landed. They began chanting *Fight! Fight!* I wasn't sure if they were egging Ryan and Jankowski on or calling for others to come and watch. Ryan held his own for the first couple exchanges, but Jankowski's size and strength were overwhelming. Ryan's left ear was already red from the battering. He sank to one knee, his own punches lifeless now and without snap. Jankowski was holding him up with one hand, the other like a piston as he punched downward, catching Ryan above his left eyebrow again, and again, and again.

I pictured myself leaving Sean's side and crossing the distance to the fighters. I'd grab Jankowski by the right shoulder and spin him around until he faced me, like I should have done in the hall earlier that morning. My punch, crisp and clean like Sugar Ray's in the Olympics, would smash the bridge of his nose, spreading it wide across his face. He'd stumble backward, the blood already flowing as I moved forward, driving home a left to his stomach, doubling him over in pain. Ryan would look at me from his knees. I'd meet his glance and nod before grabbing Jankowski by his Viking hair and shoving his head downward until his face met my rising knee. I saw it all so clearly, like watching a movie.

Standing next to Sean with everyone still chanting *Fight!*, I clenched my fists. I took one step forward but was shoved aside as Mr. Tabor shouldered past, breaking the circle. He pulled Jankowski away, the anchors on his forearms moving as he grabbed him. Ryan slumped to all fours.

Kids clapped and cheered as Jankowski was taken away, his arm raised in triumph, and then jostled me as they headed back to their seats to finish their lunches. They laughed and said it had been a great fight, that Connolly had really gotten what he deserved, that he'd be swimming naked like the rest of us now. Ryan looked up. Blood dripped from the cut above his blackened eye and landed on the cafeteria floor, the drops the color of sketched roses. He saw me staring and swallowed a few times. His Adam's apple bobbed in his throat like he was trying to get his voice to work.

"I was going to help," I said, my voice low and quiet so only Ryan could hear. "I brought trunks."

Mr. Ring, the assistant principal, came in then and helped Ryan to his feet. As he was being led away to whatever punishment the school and his father had waiting for him, Ryan turned and looked at me over his shoulder.

"*Wear them,*" he said.

I froze, afraid someone might have heard.

"Wear them," he said, louder, and was gone.

I don't know how many kids were eating in the cafeteria that day, but I felt alone as I stood in the middle of them.

I had a science test before swimming. The questions—naming the extended part of the leaf; defining the margin, midrib, and stem; identifying blade types—were easy ones that I'd studied, but my thoughts kept sliding to the book-bag at my feet and the trunks inside. Ryan's words pummeled me like two tiny fists: *Wear them.* I had survived in high school by staying out of the way of guys like Jankowski, by playing goalie outside the pool instead of fighting for the ball inside it, by swimming naked like everyone else. I knew what would happen if I walked into the showers wearing those trunks. Perhaps the beating wouldn't come in the cafeteria. Maybe they'd catch me in the deserted parking lot, or after school at the bus stop, or in the second floor lav where Jankowski and his friends smoked in the stalls, the wooden doors kicked in and splintered so many times the school stopped replacing them. The beating would come. I was afraid.

Wear them.

Science class ended. I turned in my test with half the questions unanswered and headed to the boys' locker room. My book-bag felt heavy on my shoulder, as if it contained everything I wanted to be and everything I truly was.

I undressed in front of my locker, the floor cold-puddled from the previous swim class, oblivious to the sounds and conversations around me. One by one, my classmates stripped down and drifted to the showers, some with towels wrapped around their waists, trying to stay covered as long as they could, until I was the last one in the locker room. I knew that Mr. Tabor and Mr. Jackson were already at their posts on either side of the showers—Jackson slapping the clipboard against his thigh and fingering his mustache and Tabor grinning his dead smile, his hands busy in his pockets, both looking for troublemakers, both watching for rule breakers, both of them waiting for me.

Winter Night, 1994

Originally published in *Westview* as *The Man He Didn't Kill*

Angelo stands in front of the window and watches snow blanket the deserted parking lot. He sips coffee and thinks again of retiring. The store is too much for him now. Deliveries take hours to put away, and his leg aches if he stands too long. He could spend more time with his grandchildren if he retired. He turns and faces his store, the bottles lined in straight rows like soldiers. The top shelves holding expensive items are at eye level. A tan, indoor/outdoor carpet complements the pearl-painted walls. Green signs patterned after those on the thruway hang above the shelving: Exit 5 Cordials, Exit 10 Bourbon, and by the cash register, Last Exit Pay Toll.

It'd be a good business for a young man to take over.

Headlights play across the front window, and Angelo turns to see a snow-covered Mercedes pull in front of the store. He limps to the counter, his leg pricked by a thousand shards. His right arm droops lower than his left from forty-five years of carrying heavy liquor cases high on his shoulder.

The electric bell rings as the door opens, and a man about Angelo's age enters the store. He is taller than Angelo, over six feet, his hair the same color as the snow he brushes from his sleeves.

"It's bitter out there," the man says, his voice slightly accented.

Angelo stiffens, even after all these years, at the accent. "The wind's blowing pretty good now," he answers, his voice flat, expressionless.

The man stomps his boots on the rubber mat and takes in the store. "I haven't felt a wind like that in fifty years."

"It's supposed to get worse as the night goes on."

The man removes his gloves and puts them in his coat pocket, then blows on his cupped hands. He walks past the New York State wines, stops briefly in front of the California's, and settles in front of the imports. He reaches inside his coat pocket for his glasses and begins studying the labels.

Angelo watches him.

Too many bottles have been disappearing lately, and that coat has deep pockets. He shouldn't have sent the stock-boy home early. It's not smart to be alone in the store on a night like this.

"You have a fine selection," the man says without looking up. "Some very good years here."

"I try to keep a little of everything."

"I can see that." He pulls a bottle from the rack, holds it to the light, and then puts it back. "And business, has it been good?"

Angelo shrugs his uneven shoulders. "It's always slow after the holidays."

"This weather probably doesn't help."

"Only the skiers are happy tonight." Angelo leans left so the panic button under the counter is fingertips away; the man's coat could conceal many things, and he doesn't trust him.

Angelo imagines a Luger being drawn, the fluorescents reflecting off the barrel, the explosion.

Darkness.

The man pulls bottles from the rack, studies them, and then replaces them, occasionally whispering something to himself, smiling or frowning, depending on the wine he holds.

Angelo clears his throat. "I've never seen you in the store before. Are you from around here?"

The man looks up, startled, and then turns his head slightly so Angelo can see his hearing aid. Angelo repeats the question.

"I'm visiting my sister," the man answers. "I want to pick up a few bottles of wine or perhaps a nice brandy before going to her house. You're not closing now, are you?"

"Soon."

The man wanders the aisles, stopping in front of displays and end caps, lingering in front of the clearance bin, deciding finally on a cognac, a dry French wine, and a bottle of champagne. He places all three on the counter and reexamines each label before nodding. "These will do."

"You picked some good ones," Angelo says, and the man looks pleased. Angelo pulls a cloth from under the counter and wipes the cognac before ringing it up.

"I wish I had more time to browse, but I don't trust this weather. The roads are treacherous. There's hardly any traffic. I don't know how ambulances and police cars will get through tonight."

Angelo holds the champagne, his finger hovering above the cash register. "I'd forgotten I had this."

"It was the last one in the rack. It's a good choice, yes?"

"Very good." He punches the price into the register. "From a little village outside of Vaudemange."

"You speak of it like you've been there."

Angelo nods. "During the war. I slept in a bombed-out chapel there. I remember that place."

The man smiles with just his pale lips. "We were young and strong then, yes? We could march all night through wind and snow like this."

"It was a lifetime ago."

"If you were at Vaudemange, you were in the Bulge."

Angelo flexes his leg. "I was there. You?"

The man nods.

"On the other side? The one looking back at me?"

The man nods again.

"I thought so."

The old men stare into each other's eyes, smiling queerly, as if searching for some sign of familiarity. Angelo remembers the terror, the bloody snow, the fear that his leg was gone. He remembers how fast time races during combat and how slow it drags during winter nights like this.

"I'll be damned," Angelo says.

"And here we are fifty years later, just two old soldiers. Perhaps we've met before?" The German shakes his head. "Curious, isn't it?"

"It sure is." Angelo reaches under the counter for a brown paper bag. "It sure as hell is."

He places the bottles in the bag and slides cardboard between them to keep them from breaking. "That'll be ninety-six seventy with your sales tax."

The German reaches into his inside coat pocket and smiles at Angelo, his eyes cold blue. His hand freezes as if he's deciding something.

Angelo's stomach tightens.

His finger inches toward the panic button.

The German smiles again.

He shakes his head once, then pulls his arm out, empty-handed. "Back pocket," he says, reaching for his wallet.

Angelo hadn't realized he'd been holding his breath until he exhales. The German places a crisp hundred-dollar bill on the counter.

"Thanks for stopping in," Angelo says, making change and handing it to him, hoping his voice hadn't betrayed him.

"I'll be back the next time I visit."

The German slips on his gloves and scoops up his bag. He hesitates; Angelo thinks he's about to say something more. Something should be said, Angelo decides. Something definitive and telling should be spoken by one of them. Angelo wants to understand how decades earlier, he could have been at this man's throat or frozen in his gun sights, and now they can talk about the weather on a winter night like neighbors. He wants to say something profound about fate and enemies and how circumstance chooses them.

Angelo doesn't say a word.

The German whispers, *"Auf Wiedersehen."*

Angelo raises his hand in a wave that looks like a half-surrender. The man pushes open the door with his shoulder, letting in a cold rush, and goes out into the night, leaving Angelo alone. Angelo places his palms on the counter and stares at the veins that fork across the backs of his hands and waits for the Mercedes' headlights to scan across the front window when the German pulls away. Only then does he move to the door and lock it, deciding that no one else will come in tonight, that he better head home while he can.

It doesn't take him long to cash out the register. He debates about making the night deposit. Glancing out the window at the snow now coming down in a solid sheet, he decides he'll wait until morning when it's light and he can go inside the bank where there's a guard and tellers. Angelo locks the money in the safe and puts on his heavy overcoat and the scarf his wife knitted and goes out the back delivery door.

His car, a Crown Victoria with a big backseat and deep trunk for hauling liquor cases, is parked behind the store and covered with snow. He clears off the driver's-side door so he can start the car and warm it while he brushes off the rest. When he turns the ignition, the engine sputters and coughs but does not catch.

"Come on," Angelo says, pumping the gas. "Come on."

The cold engine finally turns over, idles roughly, and backfires gunshots.

He brushes off the car, the wind pelting him with driven snow until his cheeks sting and his eyes water; he pulls his scarf higher and glances around the deserted parking lot, knowing from the war that fallen snow can muffle approaching footsteps.

When the car is cleaned off and Angelo puts it in gear, the engine falters, but he gives it just enough gas to keep it running. His back tires spin, and he pulls forward and back, forward and back, until he works himself free and fishtails across the deserted lot.

Usually Angelo listens to big-band music and the old crooners on WECK, but tonight he leaves the radio off and grips the wheel as he creeps along unplowed roads, trying to keep the Crown Vic from sliding and spinning into a tree or light post. He decides to take the thruway home to the suburbs, hoping the highway will be in better condition than the side streets, but the roads are just as slick. The wind gusts in open areas, reducing visibility so he can barely see past the car's long hood.

Cars, mere humps of snow, stand abandoned on the shoulder and median at odd angles. No taillights glow ahead of him like guiding beacons; no headlights appear in his mirrors to comfort him. His engine throbs unevenly and he feels the Crown Vic laboring.

As he rounds a curve, he takes his foot off the gas to maintain control, and sees that a car has taken the bend too fast and skidded down an embankment and into a tree. Angelo slows the Crown Vic and tries to see if anyone is still in the car.

He knows he should stop. Someone might be hurt and need his help. But it's dangerous to get out of the car in this storm. Somebody else will come along. A truck driver or plow will see the wreck and stop. Every winter the paper is filled with stories of truck drivers and plowers rescuing stranded motorists. The driver that skidded will be okay. Angelo presses the accelerator and begins to drive on, but then brakes.

What if there are kids in the car?

He pulls to the shoulder, skidding to a halt. A blast of wind rocks the Crown Vic, and he checks his mirrors, hoping someone else is coming behind him, someone who can help. Maybe he should just drive to the nearest exit and report the accident. That would be the safe thing to do.

He sits in his car for a few minutes, his gaze alternating between the wreck and his mirrors until he decides that no one else is coming. He leaves his car idling with his hazard lights flashing. The wind howls in his ears as he makes his way to the top of the embankment and, once there, recognizes the Mercedes.

"Goddamn it," he mutters.

Cupping his gloved hands, he calls down to the wreck, yelling hello as loud as he can and asking if he's all right. The wind sweeps his words away.

Angelo calls again, but there is no movement from the Mercedes. He tries to convince himself that the German has left the car and has already been picked up by a passing motorist or state trooper and been taken to safety. But the headlights are still on, and there are no footprints in the snow.

To hell with him. Let him die in the cold like I almost did.

Angelo turns towards his car, takes a few steps, and stops. He wonders if the German has grandchildren, too.

He looks up at the sky, the heavens barren of everything but falling snow, and whispers, "*Goddamn it.*" Angelo turns back to the embankment and stares as if answers can be found in the tire tracks that disappear over the side. "*Goddamn it.,*" he whispers again. "*Goddamn it to hell.*" He closes his eyes.

"I'm coming down," he finally yells, opening his eyes. "Give me a minute, damn it."

Angelo makes his way back to the Crown Vic, muttering the whole way, telling himself what an old fool he is, how he's getting soft in his old age. He retrieves a flashlight from the glove compartment. The engine is idling roughly again, so he presses the accelerator, feeding it gas until it smoothes out. Heading back to the edge where the Mercedes skidded off, he casts his beam down the slope. The blown snow makes it difficult to judge the steepness. He decides that sitting in the snow and easing himself to the bottom is safer than trying to keep his balance and walk down.

"I'm coming," he yells above the wind, pushing himself off with his arms, as snow melts through his pants and finds its way inside his boots.

Halfway down the incline, Angelo hits an icy patch covered with powdery snow that gives way, and he begins to slide. His arms flail when he tries to grab something to slow his descent, but he comes away with fists of powder that give no purchase. His heel slams into a snow-covered tree stump, sending bolts of pain ripping from the ankle to the hip of his bad leg as he comes to a stop at the bottom and cries out. Black spots dance with white flakes before his eyes. Gritting his teeth, he lies back in the snow, waiting for the pain to pass, his pants now soaked through, his flashlight lost. Breath comes in short clips, fogging the air, and he remembers that other night when he lay in the snow, his leg afire.

Angelo wipes his eyes with his sleeve.

He wonders if his leg is broken this time and pictures a crack running the length of his tibia. Snowflakes land on his face, and he tries to calm himself. His heart flutters like a wounded bird.

There's still no movement, no sign of life, from the Mercedes.

He rolls to his knees and pushes off with his good leg and balances on it. When he takes a step and places weight on his injured leg, the pain knifes through him. He bites his lip to prevent crying out again.

It's less painful to drag the leg behind him, like a piece of dead wood, than walk on it. He steps and drags his way to the driver's side of the German's car and tries the door, but it's locked or jammed, perhaps frozen, shut. Angelo brushes the snow from the window and peers in, but the glass is iced; he can only make out the shape of the German slumped over the wheel. He moves around the back of the Mercedes to the passenger's side, tugs the door until it opens, and crawls inside the wreck.

"It's okay," Angelo says. "I'm here."

Angelo eases the German back into the seat; blood streams from his hairline, covering the side of his face. Angelo takes off his gloves and feels the man's neck, searching for a pulse. It butterflies beneath his fingers.

"You're going to be fine," Angelo says, hoping his voice sounds strong.

He slips off his scarf to wipe the blood from the German's face before holding it against the gash. The man's eyes flit open, and the left pupil dilates. He stares at Angelo a long minute before speaking.

"You," he says.

Angelo nods, carefully moving the scarf to inspect the wound.

"So much blood," the German says.

"You'll live. Scalp wounds bleed a lot. They always look worse than they are. You'll need a couple stitches, that's all. You wacked your head pretty good, though. You got a hell of a goose egg there."

The German reaches to his ear and repositions his dangling hearing aid. "It hurts to breathe."

"I don't know what to do about that."

The German half-smiles. "You should call for a medic, yes?"

"We could use one. And a tow truck."

The man closes his eyes, still smiling.

"I need to go for help," Angelo says.

The German nods, his eyes still closed.

"I won't be long."

"I'll be here, my friend."

Angelo folds his scarf into a square and places it against the wound. "Can you hold this? It'll slow the bleeding."

The man presses the scarf in place.

"Will the engine start? We need to get the heater going," Angelo says.

"I don't know. It must have stalled when I crashed."

Angelo reaches across and turns the ignition. "Give it some gas."

The engine resists, but then roars to life. Angelo adjusts the heater, turns on the flashers, and presses the horn, although he's certain that no one passing by with their windows rolled up and the wind wailing could possibly hear him.

"I'll be back."

The man doesn't answer, and Angelo goes back into the storm. Dragging his leg behind him, he lowers his head to the wind and tries to ignore the pain. The snow feels wet and heavy as he slogs his way to the embankment. Looking up to the crest, the climb now seems steeper, higher. How many other icy patches wait for him? How many more stumps? He yells for help as loud as he can, hoping someone has stopped to check the abandoned Crown Vic.

No one answers. He knows he'll have to climb.

Shoving his hands through the snow, he grabs something solid—a root or perhaps a frozen ridge of earth—and once again pushes off on his good leg. He searches for a toehold with his injured one, but his leg buckles as soon as he puts weight on it, and he crumples to the ground.

He clutches his leg below the knee with both hands, trying to strangle the pain from it. Sweat breaks out on his forehead despite the temperature, and he rocks at the base of the embankment until his breathing slows and he can open his eyes. The pain nauseates him, making it difficult to think. Maybe he could pull himself up using both arms and just his good leg, but he no longer has that kind of strength. Perhaps fifty years ago he could've made such a climb, but not now, not after all these years.

He has no choice but to get back to the wrecked car and the shelter it provides. His leg can't take any weight; the pain is too much to even crawl on all fours. Instead, he crawls like a wounded infantryman, his weight on his forearms and toes, his belly down, his good knee pointing outward, his bad leg dragging behind him. Snow works into his gloves, down his shirt, chilling his skin and pinking the flesh. It's easier this time, he decides, as he pulls himself through the snow. There's no red trail behind him, no flying shrapnel above. This time he's heading towards a single German instead of away from thousands of them. He's wet and winded when he reaches the Mercedes.

The German turns towards Angelo when the door opens. "Did I sleep?"

Angelo slams the door; snow clings to his coat and hair. "I didn't get far. I hurt my leg."

"How?"

"Originally? In the Ardennes. Artillery shell," Angelo says, pulling off his soaked gloves and holding his red hands in front of the vents. "Tonight I hurt it coming down the slope."

The man presses his lips together. "I was a gunner. Long range. 170mm and above."

"Those nearly took my damn leg."

"They took my hearing."

Angelo makes a grunting sound as he rubs his hands together.

"I'm Erich," the man says, and extends his hand.

Angelo hesitates, blows in his cupped palms, and finally takes Erich's hand. "Angelo."

Erich's grip is cold, weak. "We always meet in the cold and snow, yes?"

"It's quieter this night," Angelo answers, the only sound coming from the idling engine and the heater's fan.

"*Mein Gott*, the noise. How the ground shook."

"It was those damn big guns of yours."

"And yours. And all the tanks."

"I thought it would never stop."

"But it did."

"This will end, too. Someone will see my car. I left it running with the lights on. They'll see it and find us," Angelo says, wondering if the Crown Vic has stalled by now and if anyone will ever find them. "We'll be all right."

"Yes, it always ends," Erich says, his body trembling.

"Are you cold?" Angelo asks, wondering if Erich is going into shock.

"Not as cold as in the Ardennes," he says, through chattering teeth.

Angelo again hesitates, then says, "Here," and slides across the seat, puts his arm around the German, and pulls him close. Erich settles against him, the blood from his wound dripping on Angelo's coat.

Outside, the wind continues to gust, picking up snow and tossing it, drifting it in random places, slowly building it higher and higher around the tires and under the fenders until it blocks the tailpipe. Inside, Angelo turns on the wipers, clearing the windshield. As he holds Erich, his own body trembling now, he watches individual snowflakes land on the windshield, their exactness plain to see, before they're covered and blended with the others and all traces of them vanish into whiteness.

Auld Lang Syne

Originally anthologized in *Best Short Stories from the
Saturday Evening Post Great American Fiction Contest 2014*

Griff stood in the bedroom doorway and watched his wife count the money a third time. Val's hands trembled as she piled the fifty-dollar bills on the bed in stacks of ten. When she was finished, there were ten neat stacks on the bedspread.

Val looked up at Griff. "Five thousand," she said.

Griff nodded. He had counted it twice before she got home.

"Tell me again how you found it."

"There's not much to tell," Griff said, leaning against the doorjamb, his hands stuffed in his pockets. "My shift ended, and I found it when I was cleaning the back of the cab."

"So it belongs to your last fare."

Griff shrugged. "The envelope was under the backseat, like it had been dropped and accidently kicked when the person was getting out. I don't know who it belongs to."

"You must have an idea. A suspicion."

Griff walked to the bedroom window and looked out on the street. The wet snow was still falling as it had all evening, accumulating on bare branches and sagging power lines. The plows hadn't gone through yet, and the snow on the road outside of their apartment building was drifted in places by the wind. A car fishtailed to a stop at the corner, spinning its tires when the light turned green.

"I only had three fares the whole shift," Griff said, still watching the falling snow. "The weather was bad, even worse than now. No one was out."

"Just three? And no one was acting strange? Nervous?"

"No."

Val rose from the bed, spilling a few of the piles into a green smear. She walked to the nightstand and picked up a notepad and pen. "Who were they?"

Griff sighed, his breath fogging the windowpane. "The first one I picked up at the airport. He looked like a businessman. You know, wearing a nice overcoat and carrying a computer bag."

Val scribbled. "How old?"

"I don't know. Fifty, maybe older. He had gray hair. I don't remember much else."

"Where did you take him?"

Griff turned from the window. "Chapin Parkway."

Val looked up, her pen suspended above the notepad. "Those houses are huge."

Griff nodded. "It was like a mansion."

"Did he say anything? Did you talk?"

"No, he was texting the whole time."

"Ok, who else? Who was the second fare?"

Griff shifted his weight from one leg to the other. He shouldn't have told her about the money. He should've hidden it in the back of the closet or opened a safety deposit box.

"Who was the second fare you picked up, Griff?" she asked again, her voice louder, sharper.

"A guy at Gray's Place, that crappy little bar in Kenmore," Griff answered. "The bartender called a taxi for him. He was too drunk to drive. He sang Christmas carols the whole ride."

"Where did you take him?"

"Not far. Just in Kenmore. He paid me in crumpled dollar bills. I don't think he had five grand in his pocket, hon."

Val's eyes narrowed to hard, green points. "It could have been his Christmas bonus, Griff. Who was the third?"

"An older lady, like a grandmother," he answered, knowing Val would never let this go now. "She hailed me down on Niagara Street.

She was trying to walk home from the supermarket and got caught in the storm. She was lucky I came along. She barely had enough to pay me. There wasn't any tip."

"Does she live on Niagara Street?"

Griff nodded. "Next to that boxing gym where all the Puerto Ricans train. I had to walk her in because it was snowing so hard. She was afraid of falling. The place was a dump, hardly any furniture in there. The heat didn't even feel like it was working. Her mailbox was just an open slit sawed in the door. The snow was blowing in."

"You read about this in the newspaper sometimes. Rich people living like paupers and they have thousands stashed away in coffee cans or hidden in coat pockets." Val chewed the end of the pen. "But I think it belongs to the guy on Chapin Parkway. It had to be him."

"What does it matter, Val?" Griff asked. He heard the edge when he spoke her name.

Val stared at him, her eyes tracking back and forth, studying him. "It's not our money, Griff. It doesn't belong to us. And what if the guy on Chapin comes looking for it? Then what?"

"He won't. He may call the cab company and ask if anyone turned it in, but come here?" Griff shook his head.

"It's not right, Griff. You need to turn this in."

"This money is a gift, Val. An early Christmas present for us. We can pay off bills or get a new car. Or maybe go on a real honeymoon. No one knows we have it. It's free money."

Val shook her head; a wisp of her pinned-back hair fell free and she tucked it behind her ear. "Nothing's free. You have to turn it in tonight. I don't want this money in the apartment, Griff. I don't feel good about it."

Griff walked to her and placed both hands on her shoulders and gave her tensed muscles a squeeze. "It's going to be fine, sweetie. It may not even be his."

"Tonight, Griff."

~

Griff steered his old Chrysler through the quiet streets, his teeth chattering as he waited for the heater to stop blowing cold air. The radio was tuned to STAR 102.5, the only radio station that came in clearly; they had been playing Christmas carols since November, and it seemed like Andy Williams and Johnny Mathis were always riding in the car with him now. The lake-effect snow band that had hovered over the city had shifted south, revealing a sliver of star-dotted sky. Griff lit a cigarette and cracked his window. The white-covered roads muffled his tires, so the only sounds that seeped into the Chrysler were snow blowers being started and the scrape of shovels against cement as people began to clear their sidewalks and driveways.

The heater was still blowing cold. Griff wondered what kind of car they could buy with a five-thousand-dollar down payment. Val had always wanted something smaller and sportier. Maybe he could lease something and use the found money for the monthly payments, but he knew Val would never agree to that. Griff smacked the dash with the side of his fist, hoping that would kick-start the heater; it only made Andy Williams sing louder, and he couldn't adjust the volume. He turned off the radio and took a long drag on the cigarette.

He was keeping the money.

He'd known that even when he buttoned his coat, looked Val in the eye, and promised to turn in the money to the cab company that night like she wanted. If no one claimed it, the manager, Eddie, was supposed to turn over the money to the police after so many days, but (Griff had explained to Val) the money would disappear long before that. Eddie would lose it all at the Seneca casino, and the Indians would end up with the entire five grand. Val had only handed him his keys.

He wouldn't tell her about keeping the money. He'd hang onto it until the Chrysler's engine blew or the bills piled too high. Then he'd pay the mechanic in cash or the medical bills with money orders. Val would never know.

The lights were on at Martinelli's, an Italian restaurant where Griff and Val sometimes went to celebrate birthdays and anniversaries. He decided to pull in and have a drink, nursing it for the same amount of time it would take to drive to the cab company and back. There were only two cars in the parking lot: one mounded with snow that obviously had been there awhile, and a BMW barely dusted white. Griff was certain the heaters worked in both.

Instrumental Christmas carols were softly playing when Griff entered the restaurant, and he immediately recognized the 101 Strings Orchestra; Val owned all their holiday CDs and started playing them even before the radio stations did. Martinelli's was small, with only a dozen tables covered with red tablecloths. A single green candle and a bud-vase of holly accented the middle of each empty table. One wall of the old restaurant was exposed brick. Gas logs burned in the fireplace in the center; the mantle was covered with evergreen boughs and flaming red poinsettias.

The bar, too, was small, with just six stools. Two men, the only customers in the restaurant, sat with an empty barstool between them. The bartender placed a wine glass on the bar in front of each man, then uncorked a bottle of wine and set it aside, letting it breathe.

"The kitchen's closed," he said, as Griff approached, brushing the snow from his coat. "I sent the cook and waitresses home because of the storm."

"I'd just like a beer," Griff said, sliding onto an end stool and nodding at the other two men. He touched his coat, making sure the envelope was still safe in the inside pocket. Maybe he'd spend a little of the money on a Christmas present for Val, nothing too extravagant— maybe an antique locket or a bracelet that would catch the light.

"Don't forget a glass for Bill," the taller of the two men said, tilting his head to the empty stool between him and his friend. The bartender placed a third wine glass on the bar.

The man who had spoken was tanned and lanky with creases around his eyes, as if he had spent too much time squinting on sunny tennis courts or standing on a sailboat's prow. He wore a blue sport coat with a white, open-collar dress shirt; the initials RJT were monogrammed on the cuffs. His friend was shorter, stockier, and also wore a blue sport coat but over a red sweater with a band of white snowflakes across the chest. Gray flecked through both men's hair and the goatee of the shorter man like snow. The taller man reminded Griff of his fare from Chapin Parkway. He touched the envelope again. A watch might be nice for Val or perhaps sterling silver combs for her hair.

The taller man smiled at Griff. "Have you ever seen a five-thousand-dollar bottle of wine?"

"Five thousand?" Griff asked, the number startling him. He moved his hand away from his coat.

The man shook his head as if he couldn't quite believe it, either.

"It's a sauternes," the shorter man with the goatee said, pointing to the label. "Only four hundred bottles were produced that particular year by this small vineyard. It was a bad harvest, terrible rains practically ruined the season."

"Only four hundred bottles and Martinelli's has one?" Griff turned to the bartender.

The bartender held up both hands as if halting traffic. "They brought it with them, buddy. I just opened it. My hands trembled the whole damn time. Five thousand dollars." He shook his head. "What if I crumbled the cork in it?"

"You did fine," the man with the monogrammed cuffs said.

"No restaurant would have this vintage," the shorter man said to Griff. "Most of the wine from that harvest was bought by a single collector in Manhattan, but he died without an heir."

"The bank got it all," the taller man added. "Who knows what happened to it after that. I don't think many bottles even exist today."

"But that's one of them?" Griff asked, pointing to the wine.

The taller man nodded.

"It was Bill's idea to buy it," the shorter man said, gesturing to the empty stool with his chin.

"For five grand? I didn't pay that much for my Chrysler," Griff said. God, how Val would like a BMW like the one parked out front, even a used one with a lot of miles.

The taller man smiled with just his lips. "No, not five grand. We didn't have that kind of money twenty-five years ago."

"Bill might've."

The taller man shrugged, conceding the point.

"We all chipped in fifty bucks…"

"…which really was a lot of money for us to spend on wine back then."

"For a dessert wine," the shorter man added.

"God, I hate sweet wines."

Both men laughed a little.

"Why did you buy it then?" the bartender asked.

"Bill said the bottle would be a good investment…"

"…and worth a lot of money someday."

"I guess he was right," the bartender said, placing both hands on the bar and leaning forward.

"But you never sold it," Griff said, nodding toward the bottle.

"He tricked us," the taller man said, rubbing his chin with his palm.

"It wasn't an investment at all, at least not in the normal sense."

"We found out later we were to hang onto it…"

"…until it blossomed."

"*Blossomed*. That was the word he used." The taller man shook his head. "Who uses words like that?"

"After it *blossomed*, we were all to come home at Christmas, no matter where we lived, and open it together and have a holiday drink."

"I flew in from Miami this morning. I didn't think I'd make it with this weather," the taller man said, shivering. "My blood's gotten thin. I'd forgotten what winters are like up here."

Griff studied his face, trying to picture it in his cab's rearview mirror, pointed downward as he typed on his phone. He was certain this man wasn't his Chapin Parkway fare.

"Bill promised it would taste like no other wine we'd ever have, and we'd never forget our Christmas drink," the shorter man said, smoothing his goatee into place with his fingertips.

"We were to toast our health, the good lives we had led, and the friendship we've had since we were kids. Bill was certain we'd all turn out all right."

"Should I pour it now or do you want to wait for Bill a little longer?" the bartender asked.

The taller man turned on his stool and looked towards the window. "It's snowing again," he said. "Harder than before."

Griff followed the man's gaze. The wind had shifted again, pulling the storm back over the city. The snow was coming down at an angle, veiling the lamppost outside the restaurant in shrouded light. He could see the parked cars being covered—soon the Chrysler's dents and rust spots would disappear, all the imperfections would vanish, and no one would be able to tell the difference between his car and the BMW.

"Go ahead and pour it at least," the shorter man said to the bartender. "We have time."

"And one for our friend here," the taller man added, turning on his stool and gesturing toward Griff.

"No," Griff said, even as the bartender slid a wine glass in front of him on a holiday napkin. "I'm not part of this. You've waited twenty-five years to open that bottle. The wine is for you two and Bill, not me."

"It's okay," the taller man said. "Bill would insist. It's Christmas."

"Besides," the shorter man said, "when will you get another chance to drink a five-thousand-dollar bottle of wine?"

The three men fell silent as the bartender poured. They watched the wine flow from the bottle's lip, filling each glass in deep amber. Even after he had finished and set the bottle down, no one spoke; each man's eyes fixed upon the glass before him. In the background, a lush orchestration of "*Adeste Fideles*" washed from the speakers.

"I've never been nervous about pouring wine before," the bartender said.

The shorter man picked up his glass, swirled the wine, and held it to his nose, breathing deeply before setting it down.

"Does it smell like five grand?" Griff asked.

The shorter man shrugged. "I'm no wine expert."

"How do you know how much it's worth then?"

"Bill's cousin is a *sommelier*. He told us."

Griff raised his glass and copied the shorter man. He swirled the wine, breathed it in, and held it to the light as if he knew what to look for. No one tasted the wine.

"Maybe you should call your friend and see if he's coming," the bartender said, looking past them to the window again. "The weather's getting pretty bad. I'm not sure how much longer I'm going to stay open. I got a long drive home."

The last song on the CD ended. While the player shuffled to the next disk and searched for the next song, the restaurant was completely silent.

"Bill's not coming," the taller man finally said, his voice low as he studied his tanned hands.

The music started again. "*Coventry Carol*".

"What do you mean?" Griff asked, looking to the empty stool and the full glass of wine in front of it.

The shorter man cleared his throat. "Bill had to go to New York once a month for company meetings. He always looked forward to it, coming in from the field and seeing everyone. He was on the hundred-and-fifth floor of the South Tower when the plane hit."

"He was able to get a call through to his wife. Diane stayed on the line with him until the collapse. She heard it all."

"Jesus," Griff said, remembering the images that had played over and over on that awful day when ash fell from the sky like gray snow.

"After about a year, she decided to move back to Connecticut to be with her family. She was breaking up the house and going through Bill's wine collection with his cousin. He was telling her which bottles to keep, which to give away, which ones he could sell for her. That's when they came across that," the shorter man said, nodding to the now half-empty bottle.

The men all stared at the bottle as the sad carol played in the background. Then the tall man said, his voice still low, "He had a note taped to the bottle with specific instructions that if anything happened to him before the wine blossomed, Diane was to give the bottle to James here. He was to keep it until the wine was ready, and then we were to come home the following Christmas. That's how we found out the wine wasn't an investment. It was a Christmas present for us. The last one." The taller man picked up his glass and swirled the amber.

"Pour yourself a glass," the shorter man, James, said to the bartender.

The only sound in the restaurant was the wine being poured and Mary's lament sung *a cappella*.

When the bartender had filled his glass, James raised his and whispered, "To Bill."

The four men touched glasses.

Griff held the first sip in his mouth, letting the coolness and sweetness linger on his tongue before letting the wine ease down his throat. He tried to taste and memorize all that had gone into that simple glass of wine—the rich French soil, the ripened grapes, the relentless rains that had almost ruined the harvest. He searched for a hint of the happiness that was supposed to accompany this night, but he couldn't find any.

The men did not talk much after that. They sat lost in their own thoughts and listened to the ancient carol, swirling the sauternes and looking into their glasses as if searching for something to be revealed. At one point, the taller man leaned close to James, their heads almost touching, and put his hand on the shorter man's shaking shoulder.

Griff took his time between sips, stretching the moment as long as he could, knowing that Bill had been right—no one would forget this shared wine. Looking at the two men with their heads bowed, he marveled at how one gift could touch a person, even a stranger, so deeply that he would carry it with him forever.

Outside the wind began to howl, and Griff thought of that old woman, his last fare, and the snow blowing through her mail slot. He wondered how much had made its way inside her bare apartment and melted on the floor, leaving a dark puddle. He touched the envelope through his coat and knew the roads would be slick and dangerous; he'd have to drive slowly, taking each turn carefully, trying to keep the Chrysler from skidding off Niagara Street. Then, after slipping the envelope through the uncovered slot, he'd head home, hold Val so close he could feel her heart beating against his chest, and whisper in her ear the story of three men and an old bottle of wine.

Acknowledgments

The author wishes to thank the students and faculty of Queens University of Charlotte's MFA program for their wisdom and guidance, and especially to David Payne, who taught me the meaning of "story".

About the Author

Stephen G. Eoannou holds an MFA from Queens University of Charlotte and an MA from Miami University. His work has been nominated for two Pushcart Awards, awarded an Honor Certificate from *The Society of Children's Book Writers and Illustrators*, and was honored with the Best Short Screenplay Award at the 36th Starz Denver Film Festival. He lives and writes in his hometown of Buffalo, New York, the setting and inspiration for much of his work.

www.sgeoannou.com

A NOTE FROM THE PUBLISHER

Thank you for purchasing this title from the Santa Fe Writers Project (**www.sfwp.com**).

I started publishing because I love books. I publish titles that I would buy, and that I want to see on the shelves, regardless of genre. SFWP's mission is not about creating a catalog that the accountants can get behind. The mission is one of recognition and preservation of our literary culture.

I encourage you to visit us at www.sfwp.com and learn more about our books and our mission.

Happy reading!

Andrew Nash Gifford
Director
@sfwp

Santa Fe Writers Project